ESSENTIAL COLLECTION

N.

The
ESSENTIAL COLLECTION

#1 *New York Times* Bestselling Author

DEBBIE MACOMBER

Cindy and the PRINCE

HARLEQUIN® MIRA®

Recycling programs
for this product may
not exist in your area.

ISBN-13: 978-0-373-47274-1

CINDY AND THE PRINCE

Printed in U.S.A.

HARLEQUIN®
www.Harlequin.com

For Merrily Boone, my friend and fellow writer.

One

"Someday your prince will come," Vanessa Wilbur sang in a strained falsetto voice as she ran a feather duster along the top of the bookcase.

Cindy Territo ignored her work partner and vigorously rubbed the thirtieth-story window, removing an imaginary smudge from the glass. The pair were employees of the janitorial company contracted by Oakes-Jenning Financial Services. For four nights a week they were responsible for cleaning the offices of the corporation's top executives. Tedious work, but it supplemented Vanessa's family income so she could pursue her dream of script writing; her hope was to someday see her plays performed on Broadway. And the job paid well enough to keep Cindy in computer classes.

"You have to admit you spend more time cleaning Mr. Prince's office than any of the others," Vanessa said, eyeing her friend suspiciously.

Unable to hide her amusement, Cindy stuffed her cleaning rag in the hip pocket of her coveralls and laughed out loud. "Has anyone told you that you're a hopeless romantic?"

"Of course." Vanessa's eyes shone with laughter. She pointed at Cindy with her feather duster and released an exaggerated sigh. "Sometimes I think you, my friend, could be living a modern-day fairy tale."

"A what?" Cindy might be far more

cynical than Vanessa, but one of them had to keep her head out of the clouds.

"A fairy tale."

Cindy ignored her friend and continued window washing—her least favorite task.

"Someday...some way...a handsome prince will come riding into your life on a white stallion and rescue you from all this," Vanessa said.

Cindy shook her head. "You've been spending too much time in dreamland," she scoffed.

"No, I haven't." Vanessa perched on the corner of a large mahogany desk, her legs swinging. "In fact, I believe it's fate. Think about it, girl. Your name is Cindy— as in Cinderella— and you clean the offices of a man named Prince, as in Prince Charming. Now doesn't *that* strike you as fate?"

"Thorndike Prince!" Cindy spewed out his name in a burst of laughter.

"And, as I mentioned, you do spend

more time in his office than any of the others!"

"He's the first vice president. His office is largest, for heaven's sake."

"But..."

The idea was so ludicrous that Cindy had to choke back laughter. "Besides, he's got to be at least sixty."

"What makes you think so?"

"First, Oakes-Jenning Financial Services isn't going to make a thirty-year-old their first vice president, and second—"

"It's been done before," Vanessa interrupted. Folding her arms, she hopped down from the desk to look stubbornly at her friend.

"And second," Cindy continued undaunted, "I clean his office. I know the man. He's staid and stuffy, and that's just the beginning."

"What do you mean?"

"He's so predictable. He eats the same sandwich—pastrami on rye—

for lunch nearly every day and orders it from the same deli. He's so set in his ways that he's as predictable as Santa Claus on Christmas Eve. The only thing he knows is business, business, business. Oh, I'm sure he's dedicated and hardworking, but there's a lot more to life than slaving away in some office and making oodles of money." A *whole* lot more—and Cindy doubted the first vice president knew anything about having fun.

"What do you think about the photograph of the gorgeous brunette on his desk?"

Cindy smiled. "Nothing. I'd venture to guess that Mr. Thorndike Prince has been married to the same woman for fifty years."

"The photo," Vanessa reminded her.

"That's probably the old coot's granddaughter."

"Wrong!"

"Wrong?"

"Yup. How'd you like to see a picture of your 'old coot'?"

The twinkle in Vanessa's brown eyes told Cindy she was in for a shock. "And just where did you happen to find a picture of ol' Thorndike?"

"In the financial section of today's paper. Read it and weep, Cindy Territo." She reached inside her cleaning cart and whipped out the folded newspaper, shoving it under Cindy's nose.

One glance at the dark, handsome man in the photograph made Cindy take a surprised breath. She grabbed the paper and held it in both hands as she stared at the picture. "I don't believe it," she murmured. "He's, he's—"

"Gorgeous," Vanessa supplied.

"Young." The word trembled from Cindy's dry throat. He was gorgeous, all right; she admitted that. Rarely had she seen a more strikingly handsome man. He was the type who'd stand out in any crowd. Forceful. Persuasive. Vigorous. His face was square and serious, his chin determined. His eyes gazed back at her and even from the black-and-white image, Cindy could tell they were an intense gray. There wasn't a hint of amusement in those sharp, keen eyes, and Cindy guessed the photographer had been lucky to get the shot. Perhaps most astonishing of all was that Thorndike Prince couldn't be more than thirty-five...if that.

"Well?" Vanessa prodded.

"He isn't exactly how I pictured him."

"You're right about that," Vanessa said with obvious pleasure. "Now all we need to do is to find a way for the two of you to meet."

"What?" Cindy tore her gaze from the paper, assuming she'd misunderstood her friend.

"All we need to do is come up with

a way of getting the two of you together," Vanessa repeated. "You're perfect for each other."

Playfully, Cindy placed the back of her hand against her friend's forehead. "How long have you had this raging fever?"

"I'm not sick!"

"Maybe not, but you're talking like a crazy woman."

"Come on, Cindy, dream a little."

"That's no dream—that's a nightmare." Her hand flew to the barely tamed blond curls sneaking out from beneath the red bandana tied at the back of her head. The blue pinstriped coveralls did nothing to emphasize the feminine curves of her hips and breasts.

"Naturally you wouldn't look like this."

"I certainly hope not."

"He'd like you, Cindy," Vanessa continued enthusiastically. "I know he would. You're bright and witty, and ol' Thorndike looks like he could use someone to bring him some love and laughter. You're probably right about him—I bet business is all he thinks about. And you're so pretty with that blond hair and those baby-blue eyes, the minute he sees you, he'll feel as if he's been knocked over the head."

Cindy gave a wistful sigh. She didn't need to close her eyes to imagine her prince—*this* Prince—smiling down at her with a look of such tenderness that it would steal her breath. Just the thought produced a warm, tingling sensation in her stomach.

A frown pinched Vanessa's forehead as her eyes grew serious. "We have one minor problem, though—that woman in the photograph on his desk. I doubt she's his sister. They could be involved."

"Involved," Cindy repeated before she realized what she was saying. She shook her head to dispel the image of Thorndike Prince leaning over to kiss her. In just minutes Vanessa had nearly convinced her that with one look, the first vice president of Oakes-Jenning Financial Services would swoon at her feet. Well, it was easy to dream, but life's realities faced her every day.

"Come on, Neil Simon, we've got work to do."

"Neil Simon?"

"Apparently you've decided to turn your talent toward writing comedies."

"But, Cindy, I'm serious!"

"I'm not. Someone like Thorndike Prince isn't going to be interested in the cleaning woman who vacuums his office."

"You're underestimating the man."

"Stop it! I've got work to do even if you don't."

Although Cindy returned to cleaning and scrubbing with a vigor that had been lacking earlier, her thoughts were far from the tasks at hand. When she left the Financial Center for the dark, windy streets of Manhattan, her mind was still on the tall, dark man in the photograph. It wasn't like her to be so affected by a man simply because he was good-looking. But Thorndike Prince was more than handsome; something deep within her had instantly responded to that picture of him, had innocently, naively, reached out to him. She saw in him the elusive qualities she'd been searching for in a man. He was proud yet honest. Shrewd yet gentle. Demanding yet patient. She couldn't have explained how she knew all this. Call it intuition, but she sensed that he wasn't an ordinary man.

The December wind whistled down the canyon of tall office buildings and Cindy drew her thick wool coat more snugly around her, burying her hands in the pockets. The clock in front of the jeweler's across the street told her Uncle Sal would be there any minute. No sooner had the thought formed than the sleek black limousine came to a stop at the curb. The front door swung open as Cindy approached and she quickly climbed inside, savoring the warmth.

"You been waiting long?"

"Only a couple of minutes." Cindy gave her uncle a reassuring smile.

He removed the black driver's cap and unbuttoned his chauffeur's uniform, letting out a deep breath. "Remind me to talk to your aunt. The cleaners must've shrunk this jacket."

"Right," Cindy said in a mock-serious voice. More than likely it was Aunt Theresa's cooking that was responsible for the tight jacket, but she wasn't about to tell her uncle that.

As the limousine wove through the

New York traffic, Cindy stared out the window, too exhausted to talk.

"You're quiet tonight," her uncle commented.

"Count your blessings," she said with a tired laugh. Life in their large Italian family rarely left a moment's peace. Sal and Theresa's home was the hub of the Territo clan. Her aunt and uncle had raised Cindy as their own, nurturing her with all the love they gave their natural child. Cindy's own parents had divorced when she was too young to remember, and her mother had died when Cindy was five. She'd never heard from her father, and when she'd started grade school she'd taken the name Territo to avoid confusion.

Sal chuckled. "Maybe I *should* be grateful for the quiet. When I left the house this afternoon your aunt was blistering the sidewalk with her rant."

"What happened now?"

"She caught Tony and Maria necking on the fire escape again."

At fifteen, Cindy's cousin was already showing the potential for breaking young girls' hearts. "That Tony's just too good-looking."

Sal playfully nudged her with his elbow. "Too much like his old man, huh?"

"Right." Although he'd become a bit portly, her uncle was still handsome, and the gray streaks at his temples lent him an air of distinction.

They grew silent again, and once more Cindy felt Sal's eyes on her. "You feeling okay?" he asked.

"I'm just tired."

"How many more weeks of school?"

"A couple." Two full weeks and then she could concentrate on the fast-approaching Christmas holidays. Christmas was sneaking up on her this year. Although she'd set aside the money from her last paycheck, she hadn't started her shopping. There hadn't been time and wouldn't be until her computer classes were dismissed.

Her uncle parked the limousine in front of the apartment building in a space unofficially reserved for him. Nothing was posted to claim this curb for Sal's limousine, but the neighborhood, out of love and respect, made sure there was room for him to park every night.

The apartment was quiet. Cindy and her uncle paused in the crowded entryway to remove their coats. Cindy hung hers on the brass coatrack while her uncle reverently placed his jacket inside the hall closet, setting his cap on the shelf above the rack.

"You hungry?" her uncle whispered.

"Not tonight." Aunt Theresa kept plates of food warming in the oven for them, and Cindy and her uncle often sat in front of the TV and enjoyed their late-night dinner.

"You *sure* you're feeling okay?" Sal squinted as he studied her carefully.

"I'm fine. I think I'll take a hot bath and go to bed."

"You do that." Her uncle was already heading for the kitchen, eager for his meal.

Cindy's bedroom was tiny, as were all the bedrooms in the apartment. There was hardly room to walk between the double bed and the heavy mahogany dresser that had been her mother's as a child. The closet was little more than an indentation in the wall, covered by a faded curtain. Cindy glanced around the room with fresh eyes. Thorndike Prince definitely wouldn't be interested in a woman who slept in a room like this. Her thoughts drifted to the dark woman in the photograph on his desk. No doubt her bedroom was carpeted with Oriental rugs and decorated with a fancy brass bedroom set. Perhaps there was even a fireplace.... Cindy sighed and sat on the corner of her bed feeling the hopelessness of it all. Vanessa had told her it was time to dream a little, and that was exactly what Cindy planned to do: she was going to save this special feeling she had for Thorndike Prince to savor in her dreams.

After luxuriating in a tub filled with hot soapy water, Cindy fell into a deep, natural sleep.

The following day she managed not to think about Vanessa's crazy schemes during any of her classes. Nor did she allow thoughts of Prince to invade her mind while she hurried home from school and changed into her work clothes. However, the minute she stepped into the Oakes-Jenning Financial Services building, Cindy was assaulted on all sides by fantasies she had no right to entertain.

"Hi," Vanessa muttered as she checked the supplies on her cleaning cart.

"What's wrong with you?" Of the pair, Vanessa was usually the one with the ready smile and quick conversation.

"Traffic was a nightmare."

"Hey, this is New York. What do you expect?"

"A bit of sympathy would come in handy."

"Poor Vanessa. Poor, poor Vanessa." Soothingly, Cindy stroked her friend's arm. "Did that help?"

"A little," she grumbled, leading the way to the service elevator. They rode it to the main floor, then transferred to the passenger one. Bob Knight, the security officer who guarded the front entrance, waved as they continued through the foyer.

Cindy leaned her weight against the back of the elevator as the door glided silently shut. She was concerned about cleaning Thorndike's office. The room would never be the same to her again. She couldn't empty his garbage without wondering what was happening in his life and knowing she'd never be part of it.

"Hey, did you see that?" Vanessa cried excitedly, making a futile attempt to stop the elevator as it began to rise.

"See what?" Cindy was instantly alert.

The moment the elevator hit the thirtieth floor, Vanessa pushed the button that sent them back down.

"Vanessa, what's going on?"

"Give me a minute and I'll tell you."

"Tell me what?" Cindy chuckled at the way her friend bit her bottom lip. "Have you discovered the secret to peace and goodwill for all mankind?"

As soon as the doors opened, Vanessa grabbed Cindy's arm and jerked her out of the elevator. "Look at this!" she said, shoving her friend toward a large notice board.

"Look at what?" The only thing she could see was information about some type of party.

"Read it out loud," Vanessa said impatiently.

Shrugging, Cindy complied. "The Oakes-Jenning Christmas Ball, 7:30 p.m., Saturday, December 12. Hotel St. Moritz, Grand Ballroom. By invitation only."

"Well?" Vanessa's arched her eyebrows devilishly.

"Well, what?" Gradually the answer seeped into Cindy's perplexed brain. "You're nuts! You couldn't possibly mean I should—"

"It's the perfect chance to get you two together."

"But..." So many objections crowded

Cindy's mind that she couldn't express them all. The first one to untwist itself from her tongue was the most obvious. "I don't have an invitation."

"Hey, there are ways—"

"Forget it!" Cindy hoped she'd said it with enough force to cancel all further argument. She stepped back into the elevator and waited for Vanessa to join her.

"I'm not going to forget it and neither are you. It's fate…kismet. I knew it the minute I saw Thorndike Prince's picture in the paper and so did you, so don't try to argue with me."

"I'm not arguing," Cindy told her calmly. "I simply refuse to discuss it."

"But why?"

Faking a yawn, Cindy brought her hand to her mouth, then glanced conspicuously at her watch.

"All right, all right, I get the message," Vanessa said under her breath. "But you aren't kidding me one bit.

You're dying to attend that Christmas Ball."

Was she? Cindy asked herself as the night progressed. Dusting Mr. Prince's outer office granted her the solitude to think about the magic of a Christmas ball, and she realized her friend was right once again. Cindy had never thought of herself as transparent, but she would gladly have submitted to the taunts of two ugly stepsisters for the chance to attend such a gala event. Only she didn't have any stepsisters, ugly or not, and she wasn't Cinderella. But a ball…the Christmas Ball… Nowhere else would she have the opportunity to introduce herself to her prince and be accepted as his equal.…

She ran her feather duster across his secretary's desk, and for the first time since she'd been hired by the janitorial company, Cindy wondered about the woman who spent so much of her day with Thorndike Prince. Ms. Hillard rarely let anything go to waste. Even discarded pieces of paper were neatly trimmed into scratch pads, stapled together at the top corners. The woman's theme appeared to be Waste Not, Want Not.

Cindy spent a bare minimum of time in Mr. Prince's office. The room required a dusting now and then and an occasional vacuuming, but other than that, it was surprisingly neat, which was something she couldn't say about the other executives' quarters. Emptying his garbage, she smiled as she noticed the name The Deli Belly, the delicatessen from which Thorndike ordered his lunch. He was apparently a creature of habit, but then they all were, weren't they?

As Cindy moved from one office to the next, she tried to contain her thoughts, but the image of a crystal ball dangling from the ballroom ceiling and the room full of dancing couples kept flitting into her mind. In every image, Cindy and her prince were at the center of the Grand Ballroom, arms entwined around each other.

"Well?" Vanessa said, startling Cindy.

She recovered quickly. "Well, what?"

"Have you been thinking about the ball?"

"It's not going to work." It was a measure of her fascination with Thorndike Prince that she'd even given the matter a second thought. But Vanessa's scheme was impossible from beginning to end.

"It'll work," Vanessa said with blind optimism.

"Then where's my fairy godmother?"

With a saucy grin, Vanessa polished

her nails against her cotton shirt. "Hey, you're looking at her."

"And my coach led by two perfectly matched white horses. And how about turning mice into footmen? Have you got that trick up your sleeve as well?"

For a moment Vanessa looked concerned, then she smiled and flexed her fingers. "I'm working on it."

"Are you working on a gown, too?"

"Sure…"

"If I were a fairy godmother, I'd tackle the invitation business right away."

For the first time Vanessa seemed daunted. "I didn't realize this was going to be so complicated."

"And that's just the beginning." Cindy turned back to her cart, pushing it down the wide hallway, humming as she went. It was nice to dream, but that was all it would ever be—a dream.

Cindy picked up the green metal

garbage can of the assistant to the third vice president and dumped its contents into the large plastic bag on the end of her cart. As she did, a flash of gold caught her eye. Out of curiosity, she reached for it, and when she read the gilt print, her heart rushed to her throat.

Holding the paper in both hands, she walked out of the room in a daze. "Vanessa!" she cried. "Vanessa, hurry. I don't believe it…."

Her partner met her in the hallway. "What is it?"

"Look." Reverently, she handed the folded piece of heavy paper to her friend.

"It's an invitation to the ball," Vanessa whispered, raising round, shocked eyes to meet Cindy's. "Wow!" She waved an imaginary wand over Cindy's head. "Did you feel the fairy dust?"

"It's coming down like rain, my

friend." Cindy shook her head in wonder.

"Where did you find it?"

"In the garbage."

"You've got to be kidding!"

Cindy shook her head again. "They must've been sent out last week."

"And apparently Ms. Reynolds has decided not to attend, in which case you will humbly accept in her place."

"But—"

"It's fate! Surely you're not going to argue with me *now!*"

"No." Cindy was more than willing to accept this unexpected gift. She'd attend the ball and satisfy her curiosity regarding Thorndike Prince. She'd indulge herself this once—and only this once.

On the evening of December 12, Cindy's stomach was a mass of nerves. Her cousin Tony knocked on

her bedroom door and called, "Vanessa's here."

"Okay, tell her I'll be right out."
Squaring her shoulders, Cindy forced
herself to smile and walked into the
living room, where her family and
Vanessa were waiting.

Her friend stood as Cindy entered
the room. "Oh, Cindy, you're...beau-
tiful."

Cindy's aunt dabbed the corner of
one eye and murmured something
in Italian. "She looks just like her
mother."

Vanessa didn't seem to hear her.
"Where did you ever find such an el-
egant dress?" The floor-length pale
blue taffeta grown had an off-the-
shoulder neckline and a fitted bodice
with a full ruched skirt.

"Do you like it?" Slowly she whirled
around, letting Vanessa view the full
effect.

"I'm speechless."

For Vanessa, that was saying something. Cindy's gaze rested lovingly on her aunt.

Aunt Theresa lifted her hand in mock salute. "It was nothing...an early Christmas gift."

"She made it?" Vanessa gasped.

"I sewed it," Theresa said, "with loving fingers."

"Where'd you get the purse?"

Cindy lifted the small pearl-beaded clutch. "My aunt Sofia."

"And the combs?"

Cindy's hands flew to her hair, held in place with pearl combs. "Those were my mother's."

"You look more like a fairy tale princess than anyone I've ever seen. I don't know what to say."

"For once," Cindy laughed.

Vanessa walked around her, studying every detail.

"How are you getting to the ball?"

"My uncle's dropping me off and picking me up later."

"Excellent plan."

"Listen." Suddenly Cindy's nerve abandoned her. She was living her dream just as she'd always wanted, but something deep inside her was screaming that she was being a fool— a romantic fool, but a fool nonetheless. "I'm not sure I'm doing the right thing. Sheila will probably be there." On close examination of the brunette in the photograph on Thorndike's desk, Cindy and Vanessa had seen the woman's bold signature across the bottom of the picture.

"She might," Vanessa agreed. "But you'll do fine." She tossed another imaginary sparkling of fairy dust in Cindy's direction. "The enchantment is set, so don't worry."

"What? Me worry?" Cindy said, crossing her eyes and twisting her face.

Everyone laughed, nearly drowning

out the honking from the limousine in the street below.

"You ready?" Aunt Theresa asked, draping a warm shawl around Cindy's shoulders.

"Ready as I'll ever be," she said, expelling a deep breath.

Uncle Sal was standing beside the limousine, holding open the back door. "Where to, miss?" he asked in a dignified voice that nearly dissolved Cindy in giggles.

She climbed into the back and realized that this was the first time she'd ever been seated there. "Hey, this is nice," she called, running her hands along the smooth velvet cushion.

"We have one problem," her uncle informed her, meeting her gaze in the rearview mirror.

"What's that?"

"I'm sorry, kiddo, but I've got to have the limo to pick up the Buckhardt party before one."

"That won't be a problem," Cindy returned cheerfully. "Cinderella's supposed to leave the ball before midnight anyway."

Two

Bored, Thorne Prince stood in the farthest corner of the ballroom, a look of studied indifference on his face. He idly held a glass of champagne. He hated these sorts of functions; they were a waste of time. He'd been obligated to attend this Christmas party, but he held out little hope of enjoying it. To complicate matters, Sheila couldn't attend with him. She, at least, would've made the evening tolerable. Hoping he wasn't being too obvious, Thorne glanced at his gold watch and wondered if anyone would notice if he slipped away.

"Prince, old boy, good to see you." Rutherford Hayden stepped toward him and slapped him on the back.

Thorne's response was a grim smile. He had no use for the man who was trying to ingratiate himself by means other than job skills and performance.

"Fine party."

"Yes." If he hoped to engage Thorne in long-winded conversation, he was going to be disappointed.

A moment of awkward silence passed during which Thorne did nothing to ease the tension. Rutherford paused and cleared his throat. "I've been giving some thought to your suggestion regarding the Hughes account, and I—"

"It was an order, not a suggestion." Thorne frowned. Hayden was going to trap him into talking business, and he'd be stuck with this inept

bore half the night. Refusing his over-
tures would only heighten the growing dislike between them. In spite of
his incompetence, Hayden had the ear
of Paul Jenning, the company president. Apparently they'd been high-
school friends and on occasion played
golf together.

"I'm back," Cindy said, feigning
breathlessness as she approached
Thorne. She gazed at him with wide,
adoring eyes. "Thank you for holding
my champagne." She took the glass
from his lifeless hand and turned her
attention to Hayden. "It's good to see
you again, Ruffie." She deliberately
used the nickname she knew he hated.
A woman didn't empty a man's waste-
paper basket for a year without learning *something* about him. Cindy was a
silent witness to the habits, likes and
dislikes of all the occupants of the executive offices.

Rutherford Hayden turned from

Cindy to Thorne, then back to her again. "I'm afraid I don't recall your name."

"Cindy," she said, offering him her hand. He shook it politely, and Cindy fluttered her lashes to dazzling effect.

"'Ruffie'?" Thorne asked, cocking one eyebrow.

"Yes, well…" Rutherford looked at the couples dancing on the ballroom floor. "I won't keep you. We can discuss this Hughes matter another time."

"Good idea." Thorne knew from the way Hayden's eyes were scanning the crowd that he'd move on to easier prey.

"Good seeing you again, Tami."

"Cindy," she corrected, taking a sip of the champagne. She smiled beguilingly up at the irritating man.

As soon as Hayden was out of earshot, Cindy handed the glass back to Thorne.

"Now," she said, her eyes twinkling. "I won't disturb you any longer," she murmured sweetly. "You can get back to your pouting. But you really shouldn't, you know—it causes age lines."

Thorne's mouth sagged open with complete astonishment. "'Pouting'?"

"It's true," she said without blinking. "You're a disappointment to me, Thorndike Prince."

Thorne hadn't the foggiest notion who this young woman was, but he gave her points for originality. "I'm devastated to hear it."

"I'm sure." She decided that if he didn't have the common sense to recognize her as his Cinderella, there was nothing she could do about it.

"Just who *are* you?"

"If you haven't figured it out yet, then we're in worse shape than I thought."

"Cindy who?" He studied her

closely and couldn't recall ever meeting her.

"You should know."

"We've met?"

"Sort of…" Cindy hedged, her nerve flagging. "All right, since you're obviously not who I thought you were, I guess it won't do any harm to tell you. I'm Cinderella, but unfortunately, you're not my prince—you're much too cynical."

"Cinderella?" Thorne felt laughter expand his chest and would have let it escape if she'd shown the least bit of amusement, but she was dead serious.

"You needn't worry," Cindy said. "I won't trouble you anymore. You can go back to your brooding." With that, she sashayed off, leaving him without even glancing over her shoulder.

Pouting! Brooding! Of all the nerve! No one spoke to him like that! A Prince neither pouted nor brooded!

Gradually the anger wore away. A

hint of a smile hovered at the edges
of his mouth, and before he knew it,
Thorne found himself grinning. He
forced back the desire to laugh outright. He didn't recall that the fairy-
tale Cinderella had such grit. This one
did, and almost against his will he
sought her out in the crowded room.
He saw her standing against the wall
opposite his own. Her eyes met his,
and she raised her champagne glass
in a silent toast. Her eyes were a bril-
liant, bottomless shade of blue, and
even from this distance he could
see them sparkling at him. *Alluring.*
That was the word that flashed into
Thorne's mind. She was the most ap-
pealing woman he'd seen in ages.

From the way her gaze held his, he
saw she was interested—and interesting. It wasn't unusual for a woman
to approach him; he was intelligent
enough to know he was considered a
"good catch," and many a debutante

would like to sink her claws into him. He knew that in time this woman, too, would return to his side to strike up another conversation. He'd play it cool, but given sufficient incentive he'd forgive her for insulting his pride. Although she was right; he *had* been pouting. But brooding—now that was going too far.

For her part, Cindy was acutely disappointed in Thorndike Prince. He was everything she'd expected and nothing she'd hoped. A contradiction in terms, she realized, but she could find no other way to describe her feelings. He was so cynical—as though the beauty of this lovely evening and the Christmas season left him untouched. For hours she'd been studying him. At first she'd been captivated. Only later did her fascination begin to dim. Whimsically, she'd built him up in her mind, and he'd fallen far short of her expectations. He was her prince. Her hero. The man of her dreams. She'd imagined him gallant and exciting and had found him bored and cynical. Twice he'd looked at his watch and once...once, he'd even had the audacity to *yawn*. Life seemed so predictable and mundane to Thorndike Prince.

In spite of her disappointment, she refused to waste this precious evening. She'd announced who she was. Mission accomplished. She'd better forget about her prince, but there wasn't any reason not to enjoy the ball. Cindy intended to have a marvelous time and not surprisingly she did just that as she mingled with the guests, matching names to faces. Feeling a bit smug because she knew their secrets and they knew none of hers, she danced, nibbled on the hors d'oeuvres and tapped the toe of her high-heeled shoe to the beat of the orchestra music.

* * *

An hour. Thorne had been waiting an hour for the mysterious Cinderella to return, but she'd stayed on the other side of the ballroom. Except for the silent toast she'd given him earlier, she'd granted him little more than a disinterested glance now and then. Once, she'd danced with James Barney, a young executive, and Thorne had been hard-pressed not to cross the room and inform her that Barney was no prince! But the thought of taking that kind of action was so utterly irrational, Thorne was stunned that he'd ever entertained it.

At one point, the sound of her laughter drifted over to him, and Thorne was sure he'd never heard anything more musical. She intrigued him. He discovered he couldn't stop watching her. An unreasonable anger began to build inside him when she danced with two other men.

Finally, when he could tolerate it no longer, Thorne reached for a glass of champagne and marched across the room.

"I think you should explain yourself," he said without preamble.

At first Cindy seemed too shocked to speak. "I beg your pardon?"

"I'll have you know, I never brood." Her blue eyes gleamed like sapphire as a smile raised her mouth in the most sensuous movement he'd ever witnessed. "And this business about being Cinderella—that's going a bit overboard, don't you think?"

"No, but please call me Cindy. Cinderella's such an outdated name."

She laughed then, the sweet, musical laugh that had fascinated him earlier. He stared at her, unable to look away. It took all his restraint not to pull her into his arms. He didn't completely understand his reaction—he hadn't drunk *that* much champagne. "Would you like to dance?" he asked.

She nodded, and Thorne escorted her onto the floor, his hand at the small of her back. Then he turned her into his embrace, holding her at arm's length, almost afraid of what would happen if he brought her body against his. Maybe she'd disappear, vanish into thin air. He half expected to wake up from this trance and find the entire company staring at him while he whirled around the room all alone.

Although Thorne maintained the pretense of dancing, all his concentration was focused on merely looking at his intriguing partner. On closer inspection he found her to be truly lovely; she was more than pretty, she was beautiful. Innocent yet enticing. Her skin looked as soft as silk and felt as warm as a summer's day. He didn't dare think about what that marvelous mouth would taste like. He resisted the instinct to bring her closer, although their movements were awkward and strangely out of sync.

Finally Cindy stopped dancing and dropped her arms. She shook her head. In the space of a few hours, her prince had managed to shatter every illusion she'd dared to form about him. "Not only are you a terrible disappointment to me, but you can't dance worth a darn." She stared at him, defying him to disagree with her.

Thorne didn't—she was right. Without saying a word, he brought her back into his arms, but this time he held her the way he'd wanted to from the first, pressing her body intimately to his.

Cindy slipped her arms around his neck and laid her head along the line of his jaw. The music was a favorite Christmas melody, and her eyes drifted shut as she wrapped herself in the enchantment of the song.

They moved as though they'd spent a lifetime practicing together for this one night. No man had ever seemed more in command as Thorne led Cindy from one end of the dance floor to the other without missing a step, guiding, leading, dictating every action.

"Do you always hum along with the music?" Thorne asked unexpectedly.

Cindy's eyes flew open and she nearly stumbled over his feet as her step faltered. "I'm sorry...I didn't realize."

Thorne chuckled; he cradled the back of her head and urged her temple to its former position against his jaw. "You were only slightly off-key," he murmured.

Cindy could feel him smile and she relaxed, not wanting to disturb the wonder of the moment.

Maybe she'd been wrong. Maybe, just maybe, he could be her prince after all. Thorne was holding her just as she'd dreamed and judging by the way his arms tightened around her at the end of the song, it felt as though he didn't want to let her go.

"Would it be selfish to request another dance?"

"Cinderella's prince did," Cindy whispered.

"Then I should, don't you think?"

It was all Cindy could do to nod. They danced again and again and again, neither speaking, each savoring the delight of being held. The only thought in Thorne's mind was the woman in his arms.

The only thought in Cindy's was that fairy tales could come true; she was living one.

"You say I'm a disappointment?" he ventured as the dance ended and the orchestra took a break. He had to discover everything he could about her.

Cindy lifted her head. "Not anymore."

Thorne felt the full dazzling impact of her blue eyes. "Not anymore?" he repeated, smiling despite his effort not to. "Have we met before tonight?" He was sure they hadn't; he wouldn't have forgotten her or those incredible eyes.

"Never," she confirmed.

"But you know me?"

Cindy lowered her gaze. "Yes and no."

"You *are* an employee of Oakes-Jenning?"

The corners of her mouth quivered as she tried to hold back a smile. "Did you think I'd crashed your precious party?" That was so close to the truth she quickly averted her eyes.

Thorne ignored her obvious enjoyment of this one-sided conversation. "How did you know Rutherford Hayden's nickname is Ruffie?"

"The same way I know you hate tuna salad." Cindy turned to look at the tables loaded with a spectacular assortment of salads, meats and cheeses. "Now, if you'll excuse me, I'd like something to eat."

"Would you mind if I joined you?"

"Not at all," she said.

"My mother sent you, didn't she?" Thorne breathed a sigh of relief; he had it all figured out. His mother had been trying to match him up for years. She must have searched extra-hard to find someone as perfect as Cindy.

"Your mother? No."

The honesty in her eyes couldn't be doubted. But even if his mother *had* put Cindy up to this, he felt an instant, overwhelming attraction.

Bemused, Thorne followed her through the long line that had formed at the buffet tables, heaping his plate with a wide variety of the offerings.

"What? No pastrami?" Cindy teased after they'd found a table in the crowded room.

Thorne paused, his napkin only half unfolded. "I had a pastrami sandwich for lunch. You couldn't have known that, could you?"

"No. It was an educated guess." Cindy focused her attention on buttering her dinner roll.

"An educated guess? Such as my not liking tuna?"

"No." Deliberately she took a bite of her seafood salad.

Thorne waited patiently until she'd finished chewing. "But you know me?"

"A little." Not nearly as well as she wanted to.

"How?"

"I *do* work at Oakes-Jenning," she said and pointed to the huge green olives he'd removed from the top of the dainty sandwiches. "Are you going to eat those?"

"The green olives? Good grief, no."

"Can I have them?"

Without ceremony, Thorne placed three of them on her plate, then fastidiously wiped his hands on the linen napkin.

Cindy eagerly picked up an olive and held it between her lips, luxuriously sucking out the pimento, then popping the entire thing in her mouth. She paused to lick the tips of her fingers. Thorne's scowl stopped her when she reached for another. The lines at the side of his mouth had deepened, and she noted the vein pulsing in his temple. Alarm filled her. Her worst fear had been realized: unwittingly, she'd committed some terrible faux pas.

"What did I do wrong?" she whispered. She clutched the napkin in her lap.

For a long moment, their eyes locked. Thorne had been mesmerized, watching her eat the olive. Such a small, simple pleasure, but she'd made it appear highly sensuous. He couldn't seem to take his eyes off her—or off the tempting shape of her mouth. Again he felt the overwhelming urge to kiss her. Her eyes, her mouth, the curve of her cheek. Everything about her intrigued him. For years women had used their bodies and their wits to entice him. But no woman had ever had the effect on him that this one did with the simple act of eating an olive.

"What did you do wrong?" Thorne repeated, shaking his head to clear his befuddled thoughts. "What makes you think you did anything wrong?"

"You were looking at me…oddly."

He smiled. "Then I apologize."

Cindy picked up the second olive.

Thorne's eyes widened and he groaned inwardly, setting his fork beside his plate.

The music started again long before they'd finished their meal and Cindy tapped her toe to the beat. Christmas was her favorite time of year, and the orchestra seemed to be playing all the carols she loved best.

"Would you like to dance again?" Thorne asked.

Cindy nodded. She couldn't refuse the opportunity to be in her prince's arms. This was her night, a night for enchantment, and she wanted to re-member and relive every moment of it for the rest of her life. Tomorrow she'd go back to being plain Cindy Territo, the girl who cleaned his office. But tonight…tonight she was the alluring woman he held in his arms.

By unspoken agreement they stood together and walked to the center of the dance floor. Thorne brought Cindy into his arms, holding her close, savoring the way she felt, inhaling her fresh, delicate scent, reveling in the warmth of her nearness. He felt as if he were a hundred years old in ways she knew nothing about and, conversely, that he'd just turned twenty-one. She did this to him and he didn't have an inkling why.

Thorne's arms tightened around her, anchoring her against him. His hands clasped her waist and he laid his cheek next to hers and closed his eyes. To think that only a few hours earlier he'd contemplated sneaking away from this party. Now he dreaded the time it would end, praying that each minute would stretch out forever...

Cindy pressed her cheek to his and prayed she'd always remember every minute of this night. She planned to store each detail in her heart. She couldn't possibly hope to explain it to anyone; this magical, mystical night was hers and hers alone. She would have a lifetime to treasure these precious hours and relive them over and over.

Even when the music grew lively, Thorne held her as if it were the slowest dance of the night. He wanted to kiss her so badly he was forced to inhale deep breaths to restrain his desire. Thorndike Prince did not make a spectacle of himself on the dance floor for any reason. However he soon discovered that the temptation was too strong. Her nearness was more than any man could resist and he turned his head ever so slightly and ran his mouth along her ear.

Cindy sighed with pleasure and moved her hands to the back of Thorne's neck, drawing her fingers through his thick dark hair. When his lips sought the hollow of her throat, she groaned.

Unexpectedly Thorne dropped his arms and reached for her hand. "Let's get out of here," he said in a voice that sounded unlike his own.

He led her off the ballroom floor as though he couldn't leave fast enough. "Did you bring a coat?"

"A shawl."

Irritably he held out his hand. "Give me your ticket."

Her fingers shook as she opened the beaded clutch and retrieved the small tab. "Where…where are we going?"

He sounded almost angry, certainly impatient. "Anywhere but here," he mumbled.

He left her then and Cindy stood alone, pondering the strangeness of his actions. She wanted to ask him more, longed to know why he'd insisted on leaving so abruptly. But when he returned she said nothing, following him silently as he escorted

her out of the ballroom and into the
hallway, where the elevators were.

A male voice called out to them.
"Thorne, you're not going, are you?"

Cindy turned around, but Thorne
applied pressure to her back, direct-
ing her forward.

"That man was talking to you."

"I have no desire to talk to anyone,"
he said stiffly, guiding her into the
crowded elevator. They stepped off at
the ground floor and Thorne took her
to the entrance of the hotel.

The doorman came forward. "Taxi,
sir?"

Thorne glanced at Cindy. "No,
thanks." He grabbed her hand and
they hurried across the busy street to
the paved pathway that led to the in-
terior of Central Park.

"Thorne," Cindy whispered. "Why
are you so angry?"

"Angry?" He paused in front of the
large fish pond.

The moon beamed silvery rays all around them, and Cindy could see that his face was intent, his mouth bracketed with harsh lines. His gray eyes were narrowed and hard, yet when they rested on her she saw them soften.

"I'm not angry," he said at last, his breathing labored. "I'm…" He rammed his hands into his pockets. "You're right, I am angry, but not at you."

"Then who?"

He shook his head and his eyes grew warm as he studied her up-turned face. Almost as if he were in a trance, Thorne pulled one hand from his pocket and cupped her chin, staring at her with a thoroughness that brought a rush of color to her cheeks. "You're so beautiful," he whispered with a reverence that made his voice tremble.

Cindy lowered her eyes.

His grip tightened almost imperceptibly. "It's true," he continued. "I've never known anyone as lovely."

"Why did you bring me here?"

Thorne expelled his breath, and his words were an odd mixture of anger and wonder. "For the most selfish of reasons. I wanted to kiss you."

Cindy's questioning gaze sought his. "Then why haven't you? Cinderella's waiting."

He smiled then. "You're taking this prince stuff seriously, aren't you?"

"Very."

He slid his thumb across her bottom lip, his eyes pensive. "I've never experienced anything like this."

"Me neither." It was important that he know these feelings were as much a shock to her. Despite her fantasy, despite her hopes, she hadn't expected this to happen, hadn't believed it ever would. When she'd first seen him, her disappointment had been acute.

But all of that had changed the moment he'd come to her and asked her to dance. From that time forward he'd been magically transformed into the prince who'd dominated her dreams for weeks. He was everything she'd imagined and a thousand things more.

"I haven't any right," he said, but his mouth inched toward hers as though he wanted her to stop him.

She couldn't—not when she longed for his kiss the way she did; not when every part of her was crying out for the taste of his mouth on hers.

The ragged beat of his heart echoed her own as Cindy flattened her hands against his chest and slowly, deliberately, tilted her face to receive his kiss. They were so close their breath mingled. Cindy stood on tiptoe as Thorne gently lowered his lips to hers. His mouth was firm and so tender that Cindy felt a tear form at the corner of her eye. Their mouths clung, and

Cindy's hands crept up to rest on his shoulders.

"So sweet, so very sweet," Thorne groaned and buried his face in the slope of her neck. "I knew it would be like this. I knew it would be this sweet." His breathing was uneven.

Cindy felt shocked into speechlessness. Her whole body went numb, tingling with wonder. As difficult as it was, she resisted the urge to raise her fingers to her lips. Thorne looked equally shaken. They broke apart and Cindy teetered for a moment until she found her balance.

Their eyes met for a timeless second. When Thorne reached for her, Cindy walked willingly into his arms. Then his mouth was on hers, twisting, turning, tasting, testing as if he had to reexperience these sensations. As if he hadn't believed they could be real.

When he released her, Cindy was weak and trembling. She looked up at Thorne and saw that he was unnaturally pale.

Thorne took a step back and removed his heavy coat. Gently, he draped it over her shoulders, his hands lingering there. "You're cold," he whispered.

"No," she murmured, shaking her head. "It's not the cold. It's you—you make me tremble."

"Feel what you do to me." He took her hand and placed it over his pounding heart. A frown drove his dark brows together. "I'm no inexperienced schoolboy. What's happening to me—to us?"

Cindy smiled and pressed a soft kiss to the corner of his mouth. "Magic, I think."

"Black magic?" He regarded her suspiciously, but his eyes were smiling.

"No, this is the very best kind."

He agreed. Nothing that felt this

good could be wrong. He slipped his arm around her shoulders and led her to one of the many benches that faced the pond.

Silently they sat together, neither speaking, neither needing words. Thorne continued to hold her, simply because letting her go was unthinkable. His mind spun with a hundred questions. He prayed she was a secretary so he could make her *his* secretary. He didn't care what strings he had to pull; he wanted her working with him. Ms. Hillard was planning to retire, and the thought of greeting each day with Cindy was enough to— He *was* going crazy. The cardinal rule in any office was never to become romantically involved with a colleague or an employee.

He must have given her a startled look because Cindy's eyes softened with such compassion that Thorne could barely breathe.

"It's all right," she whispered.

"But..."

"No," she said and brought her fingers to his lips, silencing him.

He frowned at her. Could she read his thoughts? Was she clairvoyant? She couldn't possibly have known what he'd been thinking, yet she showed him in a glance that she understood.

"You don't need to tell me," Cindy said after a long moment. "I already know about Sheila."

Three

"Sheila." The name seared his mind. He was practically engaged to Sheila, and here he was sitting beside Cindy, madly plotting to keep her in his life. He thrust his face toward her, his mouth gaping as one thought stumbled over another. He had to explain—only he wasn't sure how to unscramble his own feelings, let alone reassure *her*. It was as though Sheila meant nothing to him. Nothing. Yet a few days before, he'd contemplated giving her an engagement ring for Christmas. He'd actually been entertaining the idea of marriage and starting a family.

His confusion must have been visible in his eyes, because Cindy smiled with such sweetness that the panic gripping him was instantly quelled.

He looked so astonished that Cindy placed her index finger on his lips. "Shh. You don't need to tell me anything. I understand."

If she did he wished she'd explain it to him. Thorne felt like a scheming hypocrite. He was nearly engaged to one woman and so attracted to another he could hardly take his eyes off her. Even now that she'd brought Sheila's name between them, he couldn't force himself to leave. He knew he should stand up and walk away. He should escape before whatever was happening on this enchanted evening could affect him. His gut reaction was that Cindy's imprint on him could well be indelible. It was crazy, the things he was thinking. Insane to want her working with him. Absurd to seriously consider getting involved with an employee. His mother would be horrified, his father amused. They'd been after him for years to settle down, but they'd made it abundantly clear that they expected him to marry the "right type" of woman.

"You're angry again," Cindy said, studying the dark emotion that crossed his face.

"Not angry," he told her. "Confused."

"Don't be."

He took her hand in his, weaving their fingers together. She had beautiful hands. Each finger was narrow and tapered, and intuitively Thorne felt the comfort she would be capable of granting with a mere touch. The nails were a reasonable length, neither too long nor too short. He supposed she had to keep them like that in order to type properly.

"Who are you?" he asked, surprised that even her fingers could entice him.

Cindy felt the magic slowly dissipating. "I...I already told you."

"Cinderella?"

"Yes."

"And I'm your prince?"

"Yes." She nodded vigorously. "I've dreamed of you so often, and then I met you, and I knew you were everything my fantasies had promised."

He made her gaze meet his by slipping his index finger beneath her chin. Studying her intense blue eyes was like looking into the crystal-clear water of a mountain lake. She was incapable of deception. Completely innocent. She was everything he'd ever hoped to find in a woman—yet had never believed he would. She was unexpected sunshine and warmth on a winter day. Laughter and excitement.

Love when he least expected it and was least prepared to deal with it. "You said I disappointed you."

"That was before. Now I know who you really are."

"Oh, Cindy." He couldn't stop himself. He lowered his mouth to hers and kissed her again, wrapping his arms around her, holding her tight. She tasted exquisite, and her lips promised him paradise. "Cindy," he whispered against her mouth. Never had a name been lovelier. He kissed her again.

Cindy leaned into him, afraid she'd wake up any minute and discover this had all been a dream.

Thorne heaved a sigh that came from deep inside him and held her so close his arms ached.

"Thorne…"

"I'm hurting you?" He relaxed the pressure instantly and ran his hands down her back and up again to rest on the curve of her shoulders. His thumb stroked the pulse that was rapidly pounding near the hollow of her throat. Reluctantly he eased her away from him. "Tell me about yourself. I want to know everything."

Cindy dropped her gaze and laughed lightly to hide her uneasiness. She couldn't tell him anything. "There isn't much...."

She rested her hands on the sides of his face and slowly stroked his jaw. "I see so much pride in you. Stubborn pride," she said. "And determination. Were you always like this?"

Thorne smiled in response. "Always, I think. My mother claims that when I was fourteen months old, I threw my bottle against the wall and refused to drink out of anything but a cup from then on. When other children were riding tricycles, I wanted a two-wheeler. I was reading by age five and not because I was gifted. My older sisters read, and I was hell-bent to do anything they could."

"Whereas I refused to give up my blankie until I was six," Cindy admitted sheepishly. It had been her only comfort after her mother had died, and she'd clung to it feverishly, initially refusing to accept the love her aunt and uncle had offered.

"You must have been a beautiful little girl."

"I had buckteeth and freckles."

"I wore braces and corrective shoes."

Cindy laughed. "You were always athletic, though, weren't you?"

Thorne's eyes clouded momentarily. "Yes."

"Something happened." Cindy could see it—a flash of memory that came so briefly another person might have missed it.

His heart hammered relentlessly. He hadn't thought about the accident in years. He'd only been a child. Ten years old.

Cindy saw the pain in his eyes and although she didn't understand it, she knew she had to comfort him. She lifted her hand and touched his face. "Tell me," she whispered in a low, coaxing tone. "Tell me what happened."

Sensation raced through Thorne. He caught her hand, raised it to his mouth and kissed her palm. "I fell off my horse. I thought I was dead, then I realized that death couldn't hurt that much. I was barely conscious. Every breath I took was like inhaling fire."

Cindy bit her lip. The thought of Thorne in pain, even pain he'd suffered years before, was intolerable. "Broken ribs?"

"Six, and a bruised kidney."

Her fingers tightened over his. He was remembering more than the physical pain—something far deeper, far more intense. "What else happened?"

He gave her a long, hard look. "I already told you. I fell off the horse."

"No. Afterward."

"Afterward," he repeated. He remembered lying in bed in his darkened room hours later. The pain hadn't lessened. If anything, it had grown so much worse he wished he had died just so he wouldn't have to bear the agony any longer. One eye had been so severely bruised it had swollen shut. The side of his face was badly scraped, and the ache in his jaw wouldn't go away. Two days later, the doctor discovered that it, too, had been broken in the fall.

When Thorne was a child, his father was away much of the time, traveling for business, but he'd come to see his son the afternoon of the accident. Thorne had looked up at him, grateful he was there. Tears had welled in

Thorne's eyes, but instead of offering comfort, his father had spoken of what it meant to be a man and how a true man never revealed his emotions and certainly never cried.

"Thorne?" Cindy prompted.

"My father forced me out of bed and back into the saddle." He'd never told anyone about that incident. It made his father sound heartless and cruel. Thorndike Sr. was neither—only proud and stubborn like his son. And a man whose beliefs had been formed by an uncompromising father of his own. Thorne paused, his eyes narrowed. "Why am I telling you this?"

"You needed to," she answered simply.

Thorne felt startled. She was right. He *had* needed to tell someone about it, but he hadn't recognized that himself. Until tonight with Cindy.

"Let's walk," he said, getting to his feet.

Cindy joined him and he tucked her hand into the crook of his elbow. "This really is an enchanted evening, isn't it?"

"Magical," she returned, her eyes smiling softly into his.

They strolled along the walkway around the pond. Thorne felt like singing, which of course was ridiculous. He didn't sing. Ever. Not even in the shower. "Do you have any deep, dark secrets?"

"Plenty," she answered, swallowing a laugh.

"Tell me just one so I won't feel like such a fool."

"Okay." She felt an overwhelming urge to throw back her head and laugh. "No one knows this."

"Good."

She hesitated. "You'll probably find this silly...."

"I won't laugh," he promised.

She regarded him steadily, unsure

she could trust him. "I still have my blankie."

"Do you sleep with it?"

"Of course not!" She was a little offended when she realized he was amused by her admission. She bit back an annoyed response. He'd shared something profound with her, while her threadbare blankie was a minor thing. "It's hidden in a bottom drawer."

His eyes sparkled.

"Thorndike Prince, you're laughing at me!"

"I swear I'm not." He gave her a look of innocence. "Tell me something else."

"No way," she vowed, a chuckle punctuating her words.

Thorne slung his arm over her shoulder. He lifted his eyes to the clear night sky. Stars filled the heavens, glimmering, glinting, glistening above the skyscrapers. "It's a beautiful night."

Cindy's gaze followed his. "Shall we make a wish?"

He turned to face her. "A wish?"

"Upon a star." She moved to stand directly in front of him. "You haven't done this in a long time, have you?"

"No." He'd seldom played childish games. In some ways, Thorne had never been allowed to be a boy. Responsibilities had come to him early; he was the only son, and great things were expected of him.

"Then do it now," she urged, throwing back her head to stare up at the heavens. She picked the brightest star, closed her eyes and wished with all her heart that this night would never end. "Okay," she whispered. "It's your turn."

He looked at her blankly. "You're sure you want me to do this?"

"Yes," she said.

Like Cindy, he raised his head and studied the heavens. "You don't honestly believe in this, do you?"

"You're asking Cinderella something like that? Of course, I believe. It's required of every princess in a fairy tale."

"What should I ask for?"

It took Cindy a moment to realize that whatever Thorne wanted in life he purchased without a second thought. He probably had every material possession he could possibly desire.

"Ask for something you never expected to receive," she told him softly.

Thorne looked at Cindy. He'd never expected to meet anyone like her. Someone so pure and good, so honest and forthright. A woman who stirred his mind as well as his heart. A woman of insight and laughter. He felt like a teenager, yearning to find a way to please her—to thank her for giving him this priceless gift of joy.

She felt as though his eyes were melting her soul. He was looking at her as she'd always imagined the great heroes of literature viewed the loves of their lives. The way Heathcliff regarded Catherine or Mr. Rochester saw Jane Eyre. The bored, cynical look that tightened his features when she'd first arrived at the party had been replaced with one of tenderness.

"Close your eyes," she told him when she found her voice. "You have to close your eyes to make your wish come true."

Reluctantly he did. But he didn't need any stars or wishes to be granted his one request. Without his even asking, it had already come true: everything he'd ever wanted was standing a few inches away from him. And if he doubted, all he had to do was reach out and touch her. Cindy was his, and he'd found her just in time. To think that only a few hours before, he'd dreaded attending this party. Now he'd thank God every day of his life that he'd been there to meet Cindy.

"Have you finished?" she whispered.

Slowly Thorne opened his eyes. "Are you going to tell me your wish?" he asked, bringing her against his side. He had to keep touching her to believe she was real.

"I might as well," she said softly. "There's no possibility it'll ever come true."

"Don't be so sure. I thought we agreed this night is filled with magic."

"It *couldn't* come true." Her footsteps matched his as they continued strolling. "I asked that this night never end."

"Ah." Thorne nodded. "But in some ways it never will."

"How's that?" Cindy turned her head to study his expression. When she'd first conceived of this plan, she'd counted on the magic of the night to work for her. Now that she saw how much Thorne had been affected by her schemes, she marveled at the power of a wish.

"This night *will* last forever," Thorne said thoughtfully.

"But how?" Cindy didn't understand because midnight loomed and she knew she had to leave him. There was no staying at the ball for Cinderella.

"It will live in our hearts."

Tears sprang to Cindy's eyes, and she hurriedly turned her head in an effort to hide her emotion from Thorne. She hadn't dared to hope he'd be so romantic.

"That's beautiful," she said in a choked whisper. "Prince Charming himself couldn't have said it any better."

"Only Cinderella would know that."

Cindy smiled, letting the wonder of the night dispel all doubts.

"So you're still claiming to be Cinderella?"

"Oh, yes, it's quite true."

His steps slowed. "Do you have two ugly stepsisters?"

"No," she answered, grateful he'd steered the conversation to lighter subjects.

"What about a fairy godmother?"

"A wonderful but quite ordinary godmother," she answered, convinced her aunt would appreciate the compliment. "But that doesn't mean she lacks magical abilities."

"Did she turn the mice into horses for your carriage?"

Cindy frowned. "I don't exactly have a carriage."

"Yes, you do," Thorne said, leading her onto the sidewalk along Central Park South. Horse-drawn carriages lined the streets, as though waiting for her command. "Your carriage, my lady," Thorne told her with a bow.

As if reading Thorne's mind, the middle-aged driver, who wore a black top hat, stepped forward and opened the carriage door. Cindy accepted his hand and climbed onto the black leather cushion. She tucked her dress around her, still wearing Thorne's overcoat. She wondered guiltily if he felt chilled, but the warmth of the look he gave her chased away her concerns.

Sitting beside Cindy, Thorne slipped his arm around her shoulders. "I've lived in Manhattan for the past six years and I've never done this."

"Me neither," Cindy admitted, feeling as excited as a child.

"I may have confused the driver, however," Thorne said, his eyes twinkling with merriment. "I told him we wanted to survey our kingdom."

Cindy laughed. "Oh, dear, the poor man. He must think we're both crazy."

"We are, but I don't care. Do you?"

"Not in the least."

The driver jumped into the carriage box and urged the horse onto the street. The giant wheels at Cindy's side drowned out the clopping of the horse's hooves against the pavement.

"I've always wanted to do this," Cindy said. "Thank you, Thorne." She laid her head on his shoulder and drew in a deep breath. She yearned to hold on to this moment for as long as she could....

Thorne intertwined his fingers with hers and raised her hand to his mouth. "I know so little about you."

"You know everything that's important."

"I feel like I do," he said. "I know this seems impossible, but it's as if I've known you all my life."

"In some ways, I think I might've

been born for this night," Cindy told him.

"I feel like I've been born for *you*."

She went still. She couldn't swallow. They had only tonight, only these few hours, and when midnight came, she'd have to go back to being the girl who cleaned his office. A nobody. Certainly no one who'd ever interest Thorndike Prince, first vice president. Her mind whirled with countless dreams and visions, but they all ended with the same shattering reality. She couldn't change who she was, and he couldn't change the man he'd become. There could be no middle ground for them.

"You're very quiet all of a sudden," Thorne observed. He liked having her close to him. He loved holding her and kissing her. But the fascination he felt for her wasn't merely physical. It was more than that. Something buried deep within him had reached out and touched something deep within her, something profound. His inner self had connected with hers. With Cindy, he experienced a wholeness, a rightness that had been missing from his life.

"Let's not think beyond anything except tonight," Cindy said. She was trying to conjure up ways in which she could meet him again, but she quickly realized the hopelessness of it all. A sadness surrounded her heart.

"We'll share every night for the rest of our lives," Thorne promised. He knew he was rushing her. They'd only met a few hours before, and here he was, practically asking her what names she wanted to give their children. The thought stunned him. He'd always been described as an unemotional, hard-hearted cynic, but he was talking like a lovesick teenager. And everything he'd said made sense. He'd been ignorant before meeting Cindy.

Stupid. Now that he'd met her, he understood what drove men to impossible feats in the name of love. He'd walk over hot coals to get to Cindy. He'd wade through a raging river. Nothing would stop him now that he'd discovered her.

"I want you to meet my family." He shocked himself by making the suggestion.

"Your…family?" Cindy repeated.

"Yes." He'd talk to his mother and father first. They'd be surprised, of course, since they'd been expecting him to announce that he was marrying Sheila. Sheila. He nearly laughed aloud. He couldn't even remember what the other woman looked like.

His parents could be his and Cindy's biggest hurdle. But once they met her they wouldn't question his actions. After the initial displeasure his mother would love her, Thorne was certain of that. His father was another matter, but given time, he'd respect Thorne's decision. Things could get a bit sticky with Sheila, but she was a reasonable woman. She always said she wanted what was best for Thorne, and as soon as he explained, Thorne was convinced that she, too, would understand.

Within a matter of hours a young woman with a saucy grin had turned his life upside down. And Thorne loved it.

"I...can't meet your family." Cindy's mind was in turmoil.

"Of course you can. They're going to fall for you just like I have."

"Thorne—"

"Stop." He pressed his finger to her lips, as she'd done to him earlier. "Here," he said, and placed her hand over his heart. "Feel how excited and happy I am. I feel alive for the first time in years. You've done that for me.

I want to laugh and sing and dance, and I never do any of those things."

"But I can't—"

"I know I'm probably going a thousand times too fast. I realize it all sounds crazy, but I've been waiting *years* for you. Years." He framed her face with his hands and he kissed her with infinite gentleness. His mouth lingered on hers as if he couldn't get his fill. "What took you so long, Cindy? What took my Cinderella so long?"

Cindy swallowed a sob at the tenderness she saw in his eyes. "Thorne, please...don't..."

His mouth stopped her. He was kissing her again until her senses spun at breakneck speed. There was no question of refusing herself the luxury of his touch. Nor was there any question of disillusioning him. Soon enough he'd learn the truth. Soon enough he'd know she wasn't who she pretended to be. She was no princess. Her family name wasn't going to gladden any banker's heart.

"I'd be honored to meet your family," she finally said.

"Tomorrow, then."

"Whenever you wish." She couldn't meet his eyes, knowing there'd be no tomorrows for them.

They had so little time together. She couldn't ruin everything now. Maybe it was wrong not to tell him she was the janitorial worker who cleaned his office and that she had no intention of embarrassing him in front of his family. But it couldn't be any more wrong than crashing the party and seeking out Thorndike Prince in the first place.

The carriage driver cleared his throat. Irritated, Thorne broke away from Cindy and saw that they'd completed the circle and were back.

"Shall we go around again?" On

this trip, he'd gotten her to agree to meet his family. He'd seen the fear in her eyes and realized how much the thought had intimidated her. Yet she'd agreed. He yearned to hold her and assure her that he'd never leave her, that with a little time and patience his family would be as impressed with her as he was.

Somewhere in the distance church bells began to chime. Cindy paused, counting the tones. "Midnight!" she cried, her heart beating frantically. "It's midnight. I've...I've got to go. I'm sorry...so sorry." She stood, and with the driver's help climbed down from the carriage.

"Cindy." Thorne reached out for her, but she was already rushing away. He ran after her. "I'll take you home. Don't worry about missing your ride—I'll see you safely home."

Tears filled her eyes as she handed him his coat and paused to throw her arms around him, hugging him fiercely. "You don't understand."

She was right about that, Thorne mused. She looked stricken—frightened and so unhappy that he longed to ease whatever pain she was suffering.

"It was the most wonderful night of my life. I'll…remember it, and I'll always…always remember you."

"You won't get a chance to forget me." He tried to keep her with him, but she whirled around and picked up her skirts, racing off as though there were demons in wild pursuit.

Bewildered, Thorne watched her race into traffic. She'd crossed the busy street and was halfway down the sidewalk, when she turned abruptly. "Thank you," she yelled, raising her hand to wave. "Thank you for making my dreams come true." She covered her mouth with her hand and even from this far away Thorne could see that she was weeping. She ran in earnest then, sprinting to the corner. The instant she reached it a long black limousine pulled up. As if by magic, the door opened and Cindy slid inside. The limo was gone before Thorne could react.

"Sir."

For a moment Thorne didn't respond.

"She dropped this." The carriage driver handed Thorne a pearl comb.

The older man in the black top hat stared at Thorne. "Had to be home by midnight, did she?"

"Yes," Thorne answered without looking at him.

"Sounds like Cinderella."

"That's who she said she was."

The driver chuckled. "Then you must be Prince Charming."

Thorne still didn't move. "I am."

Apparently the carriage driver found that even more amusing. "Sure, fella. And I'm Donald Trump."

Four

The first thing Thorne thought about when he woke early Sunday morning was Cindy. He'd drifted into a deep, restful sleep, picturing her lovely face, and he woke cursing himself for not getting her phone number. Being forced to wait a whole day to see her again was nearly intolerable, but she'd left in such a rush that he hadn't managed to ask her for it. Now he was paying the price for his own lack of forethought.

After he'd showered, he stood, wearing a thick robe, in front of his fourteenth-floor window. Lower Manhattan stretched out before him. He couldn't believe how much he felt like singing. In fact, he'd been astonished to find himself humming in the shower. He gripped the towel around his neck with both hands and expelled a long sigh. It was almost as if…as if he'd been reborn. The world below seethed with activity. Yellow cabs crowded the streets. A tourist boat cruised around the island. Funny, he hadn't paid much attention to the Hudson River or the seaport or any other New York sights in a long while. Now they sparkled with new freshness, like a thousand facets in a flawless diamond. It seemed ridiculous to be so sure he was in love, but he felt breathless with excitement just thinking about Cindy.

The phone rang and Thorne reached for it immediately. It was unrealistic to hope the call was from Cindy, yet he nearly sighed with disappointment when his mother's voice greeted him.

"Good morning, Thorne."

"Good morning, Mother."

"You certainly sound cheerful. How was the Christmas Ball?"

"Fabulous."

"Did Sheila go with you?"

"No, she couldn't get away." His mother liked to keep close tabs on her children. Thorne tolerated her frequent calls because she was his mother, and her motivations were benign, but he'd made it clear that his personal life was his own. She wanted him settled, sedately married and producing enough grandchildren to keep her occupied. His sisters had done their part and now it was his turn.

He spoke again, remembering that he'd asked Cindy to meet his family. "Mother, listen, I'm glad you phoned. There's someone I'd like to bring to the house. Would it be possible to have her to dinner soon?"

"Her?"

"Yes, if it's not inconvenient, perhaps we could set it up for Christmas week."

"Do you have exciting news for us, darling?"

Thorne weighed his words. "I suppose you could say that." He'd met the woman he planned to share his life with. It didn't get much more exciting than that, but he wasn't about to announce it to his family. After all, he'd just met Cindy. His parents would scoff at him, and even Thorne had to admit that, on the surface, anyway, he was behaving like a romantic fool.

"I believe your father and I have already guessed your news." His mother's voice rose with excitement.

"It's not what you think, Mother." Thorne paused and chuckled. "Or *who* you think. I met someone wonderful...someone very special. I suppose it's a bit presumptuous of me, but I invited her over to meet you and Dad." The invitation alone must have astounded his mother, since he rarely introduced his girlfriends to his family.

A short silence followed. "This someone you met...she isn't by chance...Sheila?" his mother asked, her voice tinged with unlikely hope.

"Her name is Cindy, and we met at the Christmas Ball." His mother would assume he'd lost his mind if he were to tell her that the minute he'd held Cindy, he'd known she was going to be the most important person in his life.

"Cindy." His mother repeated it slowly. "What's her last name?"

Thorne knew she was really inquiring about Cindy's family. He hated to admit it, but his mother was a terrible snob.

"Surely this girl has a surname?" She was obviously displeased with this unexpected turn of events.

Thorne hesitated, realizing he didn't know Cindy's surname any more than he did her phone number. "I...don't believe she told me."

"You don't know her last name?"

"I just told you that, Mother. But it's no problem. I'll see her again Monday morning." Even as he said it, two days felt like an eternity, and Thorne wasn't convinced he could wait that long. "She's an employee of Oakes-Jenning."

Another lengthy pause followed. "You haven't said anything to Sheila?"

"Of course not, I only met Cindy last night. Listen, Mother, I'm probably making a mistake even mentioning her to you, but—"

"It's just a shock, that's all," his mother responded calmly, having regained her composure. "Do me a favor, Thorne, and don't say anything to Sheila yet."

"But, Mother—"

"I wouldn't want you to mislead the poor girl, but you might save yourself considerable heartache until you and... What was her name again?"

"Cindy."

"Ah, yes, Cindy. It would be better if you sorted out your feelings for Cindy before you said something to Sheila that you might regret later."

"Cindy knows all about Sheila."

"Yes, but Sheila doesn't know about Cindy, and my guess is you should let this new...relationship simmer until you're sure of your feelings."

Thorne's jaw tightened. He'd been foolish to say anything to his mother. It was too soon. Later, when they saw how much he'd changed, they'd want to know the reason; he could tell them all about Cindy then.

"Thorne?" His mother prompted. "Do you agree?"

For a moment he had to stop and figure out what she wanted him to agree to. "I won't tell Sheila," he promised.

"Good." She sighed loudly, her relief evident.

"You must have called for some reason, Mother."

"Oh, yes," she said and laughed nervously. "It was about Christmas Day. I was wondering if you minded...if I invited Sheila."

"Perhaps it would be best if you didn't." Although Christmas was only a week and a half away, Thorne had hoped to share this special day with Cindy. Christmas and every day before and every day after.

The pause that followed told Thorne his objection had come too late.

"I'm afraid...I happened to run into her yesterday when I was shopping...

and, oh, dear, this is going to be a bit messy."

"Sheila's already been invited," Thorne finished for his mother. He closed his eyes to the anger that rained over him, but quickly forgave her interfering ways. She hadn't meant to cause a problem. It must've seemed natural to extend the invitation when he'd recently indicated he'd probably be marrying Sheila.

"Will that be too uncomfortable, darling?"

"Don't worry about it, Mother. I'm sure everything will work out fine." Cindy would understand, Thorne thought confidently. She was a generous person who revealed no tendencies toward unreasonable jealousy.

"I do apologize, but your father and I both thought Sheila would be joining our family...."

"I know, Mother. My change of heart was rather unpredictable."

The conversation with his mother ended soon, and Thorne hung up the phone, more certain than ever about his feelings for Cindy. Remembering the way she'd strolled up to him at the ball and announced that she was Cinderella brought a quivering smile to his mouth. And then she'd told him what a disappointment he was. Thorne laughed out loud. Monday morning couldn't come soon enough.

Cindy woke late the next morning, feeling both exhilaration and regret.

The evening with Thorne had been so much more than she'd dared to dream. She hadn't been able to sleep for hours after Uncle Sal had taken her home. She'd lain in bed, reliving every part of the evening. The night had been perfect—after their awkward beginning when she'd introduced herself. Remembering the tenderness she'd seen in his gaze when he looked down at her in the carriage, she felt an aching sob in her chest.

She'd been wrong to play the role of Cinderella. It would've been so much easier if she'd never met Thorne Prince. Now she was forever doomed to feel this ache within her for having so flippantly tempted fate.

When she'd arrived home, even before she'd undressed, Cindy had sat on the end of her bed and tried to picture Thorne in her home. The image was so discordant that she'd cast the thought from her mind. If Thorne were to see this apartment and the earthy family she loved, he'd be embarrassed. Thorne Prince didn't know what it meant to live from paycheck to paycheck or to "make do" when money was tight. He might as well be from another planet in a neighboring solar system, he was so far removed from her way of life.

"Cindy." Her aunt knocked at the bedroom door. "Are you awake?"

Cindy sat up awkwardly and leaned against her headboard. "I'm up... come on in."

Slowly, her aunt opened the door. Her eyes met Cindy's. "It's nearly noon. Are you feeling ill?"

It was unusual for Cindy to stay in bed for any reason. "A headache."

Aunt Theresa sat on the edge of the bed and brushed the hair away from Cindy's forehead. "Did you have a good time last night?" she asked.

Cindy's gaze dropped to the patchwork quilt that served as her bedspread. "I had a wonderful time."

"Did Cinderella meet her prince?"

Cindy's eyes glistened at the memory. "I spent most of the evening with him."

"Was he everything Cinderella expected?"

Cindy nodded because speaking

was impossible. She leaned forward enough to rest her head on her aunt's shoulder.

"And now?" The older woman probed.

"And now Cinderella realizes what a terrible fool she was because at midnight she turned back into plain, simple Cindy Territo." A tear scorched her cheek and her arms circled her aunt's neck. Just as she had as a child, Cindy needed the warmth and security of her aunt's love.

"My darling girl, you are neither plain nor simple."

Cindy sniffled and sadly shook her head. "Compared to other women he knows, I am."

"But he liked you."

"He probably thought I was a secretary."

"Nevertheless, he must've been impressed to have spent the evening in your company. Does it matter so much if you're a secretary or a cleaning woman?"

"Unfortunately, it does."

"It seems to me that you're selling your prince short," her aunt said soothingly, stroking Cindy's hair. "If he's everything you said, it wouldn't matter in the least."

Cindy said nothing. She couldn't answer her aunt's questions. Her own doubts were overwhelming.

"Do you plan to see him again?" Theresa asked, after a thoughtful moment.

Cindy closed her eyes. "Never," she whispered.

Monday morning Thorne walked into his office fifteen minutes before he usually did. Ms. Hillard, his secretary, looked up from her desk, revealing mild surprise that her boss was early.

"Good morning, Ms. Hillard. It's a beautiful day, isn't it?"

His secretary's mouth dropped open. "It's barely above freezing and they're forecasting a snowstorm by midafternoon."

"I love snow," Thorne continued, undaunted.

Ms. Hillard rolled out her chair and stood. "Are you feeling all right, sir?"

"I'm feeling absolutely wonderful."

"Can I get you some coffee?"

"Please." Thorne strolled toward his desk. "And contact Wells in Human Resources, would you?"

"Right away." A minute later she delivered his coffee. The red light on his phone was lit, and Thorne sat down and reached for the receiver.

"This is Thorndike Prince," he began in clipped tones. "Would you kindly check your files for the name *Cindy*. She works on the executive floor. I'd like her full name and the office number."

"Cindy?" the director repeated.

"Unfortunately, I don't have her surname."

"This may take some time, Mr. Prince. I'll have to call you back."

Thorne thumped his fingers against his desk in an effort to disguise his impatience. "I'll wait to hear from you." He replaced the receiver and leaned back in his chair, holding his mug of coffee in both hands. He gazed out the window and noted for the first time the dark, angry clouds that threatened the sky. A snowstorm, Ms. Hillard had said. Terrific! He'd take Cindy for a walk in the falling snow and warm her with kisses. They'd go back to the park and feed the pigeons and squirrels, then head over to his apartment and drink mulled wine. He'd spent one restless day without her and he wasn't about to waste another. His head was bursting with things he wanted to tell her, things he found vitally important to share. Today he'd learn everything he could about her. Once he knew everything, he'd take her in his arms and tell her the magic hadn't stopped working. The spell she'd cast on him hadn't faded and it wouldn't. If anything, it had grown stronger.

The phone rang, and he jerked the receiver off its cradle. "Prince here."

"This is Jeff Wells from HR."

"Yes?"

"Sir—" he paused and cleared his throat "—I've checked all our records and I can't find anyone named Cindy or Cynthia employed on the executive floor."

"Then look again," Thorne said urgently.

"Sir, I've checked the files three times."

"Then please do so again." Thorne

hung up the phone. He wondered grimly if he'd have to go down there and locate Cindy's name himself.

A half hour later, Thorne had to agree with Wells. There wasn't a secretary or assistant in the entire company named Cindy. Thorne slammed the filing-cabinet drawer shut with unnecessary force.

"Who was in charge of the Christmas Ball?" he demanded.

Jeffrey Wells, a diminutive man who wore a bow tie and glasses, bowed his head. "I was, Mr. Prince."

"The ball was by invitation only. Is that correct?"

"Yes, sir, I received my instructions from—"

"I want the list."

"The list?" He pulled out a file and handed Thorne several sheets of paper. "The name of every employee who received an invitation is here, except one, and—"

"Who?" Thorne whirled around to face the other man.

"Me," Wells said in a startled voice.

Thorne scanned the list, then again more slowly, carefully examining each name. No Cindy.

"How many extra invitations were sent to outside guests?"

"A dozen—I have the list here." Wells pulled a sheet of paper from the file and Thorne took it and counted the names. Exactly twelve. But again, no Cindy.

"Sir...perhaps this Cindy crashed the party.... There are ways," he stammered. "The hotel staff do all they can to assure that only those with an invitation are granted admission, but...it's been known to happen."

"Crashed the ball..." Thorne repeated, stunned. He rubbed a hand over his face. That was what had happened. The instant he heard Wells say it, he'd recognized the truth. "Thank you for your trouble, Mr. Wells."

"It was no problem, Mr. Prince. Perhaps if you could describe the girl, I could go through our files and locate pictures. Perhaps she's employed by Oakes-Jenning, but was assuming another name."

Thorne shook his head. "That won't be necessary." He turned and left the office, reaching his own without remembering how he got there.

Ms. Hillard stood when he entered the room, her hands filled with the mail. Thorne gave her a look that told her he'd deal with his correspondence later, and she sat down again.

For two days he'd been living in a dreamworld, acting like an idiotic, romantic fool. The joy drained out of him and was replaced by a grim determination not to allow such folly to overtake him a second time. He'd put Cindy out of his mind and his heart as easily as he'd instilled her there. She was a fraud who'd taken delight in duping him. Well, her plans had worked beyond her expectations. He slumped into his chair and turned to look at the sky. Ms. Hillard was right. The weather was terrible, but then so was the day.

Five

Thorne's violent sneeze tore the tissue in half. He reached for another in the nick of time. His eyes were running, he was so congested he could barely breathe and he had a fever. He felt thoroughly miserable, and it wasn't *all* due to this wretched cold. He'd gotten it the night he'd given Cindy his coat. Cindy. Despite his resolve, she haunted his dreams and filled his every waking thought. He wanted to hate her, shout at her and…and take her in his arms and hold her. There were moments he despised her, and then there were other times, usually late at night, when he'd welcome the memories. That was when she came to him, in those quiet hours. He'd be on the ballroom floor with her in his arms; a second later he'd recall with vivid clarity the agony in her eyes as she tearfully told him goodbye. When she told him how sorry she was, the words seemed to echo over and over in his mind.

Thorne picked up the pearl comb and fingered it for the thousandth time in the past five days. He'd kept it with him constantly, seeking some clue from it, some solace. He found neither. He'd taken it to a jeweler and learned it was a fairly inexpensive comb that was perhaps twenty-five years old— certainly of little value beyond the sentimental. Too bad she hadn't left a glass slipper behind like the real Cinderella. Then he could take it around the executive floor and try it on women's feet to see if it would fit. Instead, his Cinderella had left him something useless. He couldn't trace her with a common pearl comb.

Other than that, Thorne had nothing with which to find Cindy. The crazy part was that he wasn't completely sure he *wanted* to see her again. She'd lied to him, played him for a fool and mercilessly shattered his dreams— serious crimes for a woman he'd known less than five hours—and yet he couldn't stop thinking about her. Every minute. Every day. He wanted to cast her from his mind; then and only then could he finally escape her.

Thorne's thoughts were followed by another thunderous sneeze. He pressed the intercom button and summoned Ms. Hillard. "Did you get that orange juice?" he asked.

"It's on its way," she informed him.

"Thank you." Thorne pulled open the top desk drawer and grabbed the aspirin bottle. He felt miserable, in body *and* spirit.

Cindy inhaled a deep breath and forced herself to enter Thorne's office. It was torture to be inside the room where he spent so much of his time. She could feel his presence so strongly that she kept looking over her shoulder, convinced he was there, standing behind her. She wondered what he'd say to her—if he hated her or if he even thought about her—then decided she'd rather not know. Her heart was weighed down with regrets.

Pushing Thorne out of her mind, she ran the feather duster over his desk. Something small and white fell onto the carpet. Cindy bent over and picked it up. A pearl. She held it in the palm of her hand and stared at it. Thorne had her mother's missing comb! Cindy had thought it was lost to her forever. Not until she was home did she realize one of them had fallen from her hair, and she'd been devastated over its loss. She had so few of her mother's personal possessions that losing even one was monumental.

"What's that?" Vanessa asked, standing in the open doorway, her feather duster in her hip pocket.

Cindy's hand closed over the pearl. Knowing that Thorne had the comb gave her an oddly secure feeling. "A pearl," she said, tucking it inside the pocket of her coveralls.

Vanessa studied her closely. "Do you think it might be from your mother's comb?"

"I'm sure it is."

"Then your prince must have it."

Cindy nodded, comforted immeasurably by this fact.

"How do you plan to get it back?"

"I don't," Cindy said. She continued dusting, praying Vanessa would return to her own tasks.

"You aren't going to get it from him? That's crazy. You were sick about losing that comb."

"I know."

"Well, good grief, Cindy, here's the perfect opportunity for you to see your prince again. Grab it, for heaven's sake!"

Cindy's mouth quivered. "I don't want to see him again."

"You might be able to fool your family, but you won't have such an easy time with me." Vanessa's expression was grim and her eyes revealed her disapproval. "You told me the ball was the happiest, most exciting night of your life."

Cindy's back stiffened. The warm, fairy-tale sensations the ball had aroused were supposed to last a lifetime, and instead the evening had left her yearning for many, many more. "The night was everything I dreamed, but don't you see? I was playing a role… I was glamorous and sophisticated and someone totally different from the Cindy you see now. The show closed, the part's cancelled and I've gone back to being just plain me—Cindy Territo, janitorial worker, part-time student."

"And Cindy Territo, woman in love."

"Stop it, Vanessa!" she cried and whirled around to face her friend. "Adults don't fall in love after one night. Not true love—it just doesn't happen!"

Vanessa crossed her arms and leaned against the side of Thorne's rosewood desk. "That's not what I hear."

Cindy snorted softly. "What you're talking about isn't love…it's infatuation. It wasn't like that with Thorne and me. I don't think I can explain or define it—I've never felt anything like this with any other man."

"And yet you're convinced it can't be love?" Vanessa taunted.

"It's impossible," she insisted, although she didn't believe it. "I don't want to talk about him or that night again. I—we have to put it out of our minds." She reached for Thorne's wastebasket and unceremoniously emptied it inside her cart. When she saw the contents her eyes widened. "Vanessa, look." She picked up a discarded aspirin box and another for a cold remedy. "Thorne's sick."

"He must've gone through a whole box of tissues."

"Oh, no." Cindy sagged into his chair, lovingly stroking the arm as though it were his fevered brow. She longed to be with him. "The night of the ball," she began, her voice strained with regret, "when we went into the park, he gave me his coat so I wouldn't catch cold."

"At a price, it seems."

Cindy's face went pale, and she gazed distractedly at her friend before turning her head and closing her eyes. "It's all my fault. Christmas is only a few days away.... Oh, dear, I did this to him."

"What do you plan to do about it?"

"What can I do?" If Cindy was miserable before, it was nothing compared to the guilt she suffered now, knowing her prince was ill because of her. He'd grown chilled, which had made him vulnerable to the viruses so abundant this time of year.

"Make some chicken soup and take it to him," Vanessa suggested.

Cindy's eyes widened. "I couldn't."

"This is the same woman who sauntered up to Thorndike Prince and announced he was a disappointment to her?"

"One and the same," Cindy muttered.

Vanessa shook her head. "You could've fooled me."

If anybody was a fool, Cindy determined the following afternoon, she was the one. She'd spent the morning chopping vegetables into precise, even pieces and adding them to a steaming pot of chicken broth and stewing chicken while her aunt made a batch of homemade noodles.

"Maybe I should have Tony deliver it for me," Cindy said, eyeing her aunt speculatively.

"Tony and Maria are going to a movie, and you can bet that your prince isn't going to hand over that comb to my son without getting information out of him." The way she was regarding Cindy implied that Thorne would use fair means or foul to find out whatever he could.

"Thorne wouldn't hurt anyone." Cindy defended him righteously, and from the smile that lit up the older woman's face, Cindy realized she'd fallen neatly into her aunt's trap.

"Then you shouldn't have any qualms about visiting him. It's not Tony or anyone else he wants to see—it's you."

Cindy raised questioning eyes to her. "I'm not convinced he does want to see me."

"He kept the comb, didn't he?"

"Yes, but that doesn't mean anything."

"No man is going to carry around a woman's hair ornament without a reason."

"Oh, Aunt Theresa, I feel like such an idiot. What if he hates me? What if—"

"Will you stop with the *what ifs!* The soup's finished. Take it to him and go from there."

"But…" She strove to keep the emotion from her voice. But she couldn't hide her nervousness. If she saw

Thorne today, there'd be no fancy gown or dimmed lights to create an illusion of beauty and worldliness. No moonlight and magic to entice him. Her plaid wool skirt, hand-knit sweater and leather pumps would tell him everything.

Theresa caught her by the shoulders. "Stop being so nervous! It's not like you."

Cindy smiled weakly. She'd go to him because she had to. Her actions were mapped out in her mind. She'd already looked up his address. She'd arrive at his apartment, present him with the soup and tell him how sorry she was that he'd gotten a cold. Then, depending on how he responded, she'd ask for her mother's comb. But only if he showed signs of being pleased to see her. Somehow she doubted he would.

The television droned in the background, but Thorne couldn't manage any interest in the silly game shows that ran one after the other. They, however, were only slightly less boring than the soap operas and talk shows on the other channels. He felt hot, then chilled. Sick and uncomfortable. Sleepy from the medication and yet wide-awake. It was only three days until Christmas and he had all the love and goodwill of an ill-tempered, cantankerous grinch.

The small tree in the corner of his living room was testament to his own folly. He'd enthusiastically put it up the day after meeting Cindy, and now it sat there taunting him, reminding him what a fool he was to believe in romantic dreams. In three days' time he'd be obligated to show up at his parents' home and face them—and Sheila. The thought was not pleasant. All he wanted to do was hide in his condo and insist the world leave him alone.

He sighed and reached for a glass of grapefruit juice and another cold tablet. Discarded cold remedies crowded his glass coffee table. He'd taken one pillow plus the quilt from his bed, trying to get comfortable in the living room.

The doorbell chimed and he ignored it.

Seemingly undaunted, the bell rang a second time. "Go away," he shouted rudely. The last thing he wanted was company.

The ring was followed by loud knocking.

Furious, he shoved his quilt aside and stormed to the front door. He jerked it open and glared angrily at the young woman who stood before him. "I said go away!" he shouted, in no mood to be civil. "I don't want any…" His voice faded to a croak. "Cindy?" He was too shocked to do anything, even breathe. The first thing that came to mind was to haul her into his arms and not let her leave until she told him who she was. But that impulse was immediately followed by an all-consuming anger. He glared at her with contempt.

Cindy stood there, unable to move or to manage a coherent word. A rush of color heated her face. This was a hundred times worse than she'd imagined. Thorne hated her. Dismayed and disheartened, she handed him the large paper sack. "I…heard you were sick."

"What's this?"

"Chicken soup."

Thorne's eyes lit up with sardonic amusement. She resembled a frightened rabbit standing in front of a hungry wolf. He wondered how anyone could look so innocent and completely guileless when he knew her to be a liar and a cheat. "You might as well come in," he said gruffly, stepping aside.

"I can only stay a minute," she said shakily.

"I wouldn't dream of inviting you to stay longer," he answered, willfully cruel. He was rewarded when he saw the color drain from her face. Good. He wanted her to experience just a taste of the hell she'd put him through.

She caught her breath and nodded, saying without words that she understood.

He set the soup on the coffee table and slumped onto the white leather sofa. "I won't apologize for the mess, but as you've heard, I haven't been feeling well." He motioned toward the matching chair across from him. "I know what you want."

Surprise widened her deep blue eyes. "You do?"

"It's the comb, isn't it?"

Cindy nodded and sat on the edge of

the cushion, folding her hands primly in her lap. She clasped her fingers tightly together. "It was my mother's… You have it?"

"Yes."

She sighed with relief. "I thought I'd lost it."

"You knew very well that I had it."

Cindy opened her mouth to argue with him but quickly closed it. He couldn't believe anything but the worst, and she couldn't blame him.

"What? No heated defense?"

"None. You have the right to hate me. I lied to you, but not in the way you think."

"You're no secretary."

"No, but if you'll remember, I never said I was."

"But you didn't stop me from thinking that."

Cindy dropped her eyes to her clenched hands. "As I said before, you have every right to be angry, but if it's any consolation to you—I am deeply and truly sorry."

His gaze narrowed, condemning her. "Such innocent eyes. Who would have guessed that such deception lay just below the surface?"

Cindy clamped her teeth together with such force that her jaw ached. Every word was a slap in the face and it hurt. His eyes were so cold and full of contempt. "If I could have the comb…I'll be on my way."

"Not quite yet." He stood and joined her, pulling her to her feet. "You owe me something for all the lies you told…for deceiving me into thinking you were kind and good." For filling his head with dreams and breaking her unspoken promises…

Cindy drew back sharply.

His eyes narrowed on her flushed face and his hands tightened around her upper arms. He pulled her against him and slanted his mouth over hers.

Cindy went still but didn't resist.

Thorne felt her submission and he loosened his grip, drawing slowly back. She'd gone deathly pale, and he instantly felt overwhelming regret. He dropped his hands and watched as she took a stumbling step away from him.

"I apologize for that," he said hoarsely. He was wrong about her. She wasn't cold and calculating, but warm and generous. It was all there for him to read in her clear, blue eyes. Her chin shook slightly and those magical eyes stared up at him, glimmering with hurt. He longed to soothe away the pain he'd inflicted. Utterly defeated, he turned and walked away. "I'll get the comb."

Thorne stumbled halfway down the hall that led to his bedroom. The floor seemed to pitch and heave under him, and he sagged against the wall to keep from falling. He knew it was the medication—the doctor had warned him about the dizzying effect.

"Thorne…" Cindy was at his side, wrapping an arm around his waist.

"I'll be fine in a minute."

Her hold tightened. "You're sick."

His breathless chuckle revealed his amusement. "Are you always so perceptive?"

"No." She tried to support him. "Let me get you into bed."

"Those are misleading words, Cinderella. I'm sure your fairy godmother would be shocked."

"Quit joking, I'm serious."

He turned his head and his gaze pinned hers. "So am I."

"Thorne!" Her face heated. As best she could, Cindy directed him into the bedroom. The huge king-size bed dominated the middle of the room and was a mess of tangled sheets and blankets. She left him long enough to pull back the covers and fluff up the pillows.

Because he felt so weak, Thorne sat on the edge of the bed and ran a weary hand over his face. Under normal circumstances he would've been humiliated to have a woman fuss over him like this, but nothing about his relationship with Cindy was conventional.

"Here, let me help you," she insisted, urging him to lie down. She held the back of one hand to his forehead.

"No." He brushed her hand away.

"You need to rest."

"No," he repeated.

"Thorne, please, you're running a fever."

"If I fall asleep," he said, holding her gaze, "you'll be gone when I wake up." His mouth curved into a sad smile. "Will you promise to stay?"

Cindy hesitated.

"I'll stay until you wake," she finally said.

"Do you promise?"

She nodded.

"Say it, Cindy."

"I'll be here," she cried, angry that he couldn't trust her. "I wouldn't dream of leaving you like this."

He fell against the pillow and released a long sigh. "Good," he said and closed his eyes. For the first time in days he felt right. From the moment Cindy had left him standing in the park, it was as though a part of him had been missing. Now she was here, so close that all he had to do was reach out and touch her.

Standing at his side, Cindy pulled the covers over his shoulders and lingered beside the bed. She wouldn't leave the room until she was sure he was asleep. He appeared almost childlike, lying on his side, his brow relaxed and smooth. The harsh lines around his mouth were gone, as were the ones that fanned out beside his eyes.

A minute later, his lashes fluttered open and he looked around, startled.

"I'm here," she whispered and stroked his forehead to reassure him.

"Lie down with me," he pleaded, shifting to the far side of the bed, leaving more than ample room for her.

"Thorne, I can't."

"Please." His voice was barely discernible, hardly more than a whisper.

No one word could be more seductive. "I shouldn't."

He answered her by gently patting the bed, his eyes still closed. "I need you," he said softly.

"Oh, Thorne." She pressed her lips together and slipped off her shoes. He was manipulating her and she didn't like it one bit. As soon as he was well she'd tell him in no uncertain terms what she thought of his underhanded methods.

Keeping as close to edge of the bed as possible without falling off, Cindy lay stiff and tense at his side. Thorne was under the covers while she remained on top, but that did little to diminish her misgivings.

Gradually, so gradually she was hardly aware of what he was doing, Thorne eased himself closer to her so he could feel the warmth of her body against his. Sleep was so wonderfully inviting. He draped his arm over her ribs and brought her next to him. He felt the tension leave her limbs, and for the first time since the Monday after the Christmas Ball, Thorne Prince smiled.

Cindy woke two hours later, astonished that she'd slept. The room was dark and she lay watching the shadows on the bedroom walls, thinking. Her mind was crowded with conflicting thoughts. She should leave him while she could, with her heart intact— but she'd promised she wouldn't. No matter what the consequences, she wouldn't lie to him again.

As gently as possible, Cindy slipped from his arms and tiptoed across the plush carpet. Clothes littered the floor and she automatically picked them up as she made her way out of the room. She collected towels from the bathroom and threw everything in the washing machine, which she found in its own alcove.

Dirty dishes were piled in the kitchen sink, and Cindy placed them in the dishwasher and turned it on. The pots and pans she scrubbed by hand. She'd finished those when she turned around and discovered Thorne standing in the middle of the kitchen, watching her.

"I thought you'd left," he murmured. He'd woken to find her gone and momentary terror had gripped his heart. It wasn't until he'd realized she was in the other room that he'd been able to breathe again.

"No, I'm here," she said unnecessarily.

"I don't need you cleaning for me. I've got a woman who comes in for that."

"What's her name?"

He stared at her blankly, surprised by the inane conversation they were having. "She's sent by an agency. I wouldn't know her if I met her on the street. Does it matter?"

Cindy turned to face the sink and bit her bottom lip at the pain. With deliberate movements, she rinsed out the dishrag and wrung it dry, then folded it over the faucet. She dried her hands on the kitchen towel.

"Cindy." He touched her shoulder, but she ignored him.

"I promised you I wouldn't leave

while you were sleeping," she said,
her eyes avoiding his. "But I have
to go now. Could I please have the
comb?"

"No."

"No? But...it's part of a matching
set."

"You told me they belonged to your
mother, didn't you?"

Cindy nodded.

"They obviously mean a great deal
to you."

"Yes...of course." She didn't understand where he was going with this.

"Then I'll keep it until I find out
why you need to disappear from my
life."

"That's blackmail!"

"I know." He looked pleased with
himself. "I'll feel a whole lot better
once I shower and shave. When I'm
finished, we'll talk."

Cindy's fingers gripped the counter
behind her. "Okay," she murmured.

She hated lying to him—again—but she had no intention of staying. She couldn't. She'd kept her promise—she hadn't left while he slept. Now he was awake and so was she. Wide-awake.

The minute she heard the shower running, Cindy sneaked into the bedroom and retrieved her shoes. She'd reached the front door before she hesitated. A note. He deserved that much.

She found paper and a pen in the kitchen and wrote as fast as her fingers could move. She told him he was right in assuming the combs meant a lot to her. So much so that she wanted him to keep the comb he'd found—keep it in memory of the night they'd met. She told him she'd always remember him, her own dashing prince, and that their time together was the most special of her life. Tears fell from her eyes and her lips trembled as she signed her name.

She left the paper on top of the television. Soundlessly she hurried to the front door, where she paused again, blinded by tears. Her fingers curled around the knob. Everything within her told her to walk out that door and not look back. Everything except her heart. Cindy felt as if it was dissolving with every breath she took. She pressed her forehead against the polished mahogany door, fighting to strengthen her resolve.

Then she heard his voice behind her.

"I didn't think I could trust you," he said bitterly.

Six

Thorne's harsh words cut her savagely. With tears streaming down her cheeks, she turned toward him, all the pent-up emotion in her eyes there for him to read. He had to see that it was killing her to walk away.

One look at the pain etched so plainly on her tormented face, and Thorne's anger evaporated. He moved across the room. "Oh, Cindy," he groaned and reached for her, folding her in his arms. At first she resisted his comfort, standing stiff and unyielding against him, but he held her because he couldn't bear to let her go. His hands cupped her face and he directed her mouth to his, kissing her again and again until she relaxed and wound her arms around his neck. Thorne could feel her breath quicken and he knew he'd reached her.

Cindy's heart seemed to stop and then surged again with hurried beats. Being held and kissed by Thorne only made leaving him more difficult. She could hardly breathe past the wild pounding of her heart. She shouldn't have come to him, shouldn't have asked for the return of her missing comb. But she had—seeking some common ground, hoping to bridge the gap between their lives. But it couldn't be done. His words about his cleaning woman had proven how unfeasible any relationship between them would be.

"No." She eased herself away from

him. "Please, don't try to stop me....
I have to go."

"Why?"

She pinched her lips together and
refused to answer.

Thorne caressed her thick blond
hair. He drew in a calming breath and
released it, repeating the action several times until he could think clearly.

"You're married, aren't you?" he
asked in a stark voice.

"No!"

"Then why do you insist on playing
hide-and-seek?"

She dropped her head and closed
her eyes, unable to look at him any
longer. "Trust me, it's for the best that
we never see each other again."

"That's ridiculous. We're perfect
together." He was nearly shouting at
her. He lowered his voice, wanting
to reason with her calmly. "I *need* to
be with you. That night was the most
wonderful of my life. It was like...like

I'd suddenly woken up from a coma. The whole world came alive for me the minute you arrived. At least give us a chance. That isn't so much to ask, is it?"

A tear slipped from the corner of her eye.

"Cindy, don't you realize I'm crazy about you?"

"You don't know me," she cried.

"I know enough."

"It was *one* night, don't you see? One magical night. Another night would never be the same. It's better to leave things as they are rather than disillusion ourselves by trying to live a fantasy."

"Cindy." He stopped her, bringing his lips hungrily to hers, kissing her until she was weak and clinging. "The magic is stronger than ever. I feel it and so do you."

She leaned her forehead against his chest, battling the resistance in her heart. But she couldn't deny the truth any more than she could stop her heart from racing at his slightest touch.

"One more night," Thorne said softly, enticingly, "to test our feelings. Then we'll know."

Cindy nodded silently, unable to refuse him anything when he was holding her as if she were an enchanted princess and he her sworn love. When she did speak, her voice was hardly above a whisper. "One more night," she repeated. "But only one."

Thorne felt the tightness in his chest subside and the tension seep out of him. He wanted to argue with her; he wanted a lot more than one night— but she looked so confused and uncertain that he didn't dare press her. For now he'd be satisfied with the time she could freely give him.

He grinned. "Where would you like to go? A play? A jazz club? Dinner?"

"Thorne." She placed her hand on his arm. "You're ill."

"I feel a thousand times better." And he did.

"We'll stay right here," she countered, and breaking out of his arms, she returned to the kitchen. Catching him by the hand, she took him with her. She sat him down at the table and proceeded to inspect his freezer and cupboards.

Thorne watched as she organized their meal. Before he knew what was happening, Cindy had him at the counter, ripping apart lettuce leaves for a salad. It was as though she'd worked in his kitchen all her life. She located frozen chicken breasts, thawed them in the microwave and set them in the oven with potatoes wrapped in aluminum foil. Then she searched his cupboards, gathering the ingredients for a mushroom sauce.

Thorne paused long enough in his

task to choose a CD. Soon music surrounded them as they worked; once everything was prepared they moved to the living room. As they sat on the couch, Thorne's arm went around her shoulders and she bent her arm to connect her fingers with his. Her head rested on his shoulder. The moment was serene, peaceful. Thorne had never known a time like this with a woman. All the women he'd met wanted parties and excitement, attention and approval. He hadn't married, hadn't even thought of it until recently. He'd given up looking for that special woman, the one who'd fill his days with happiness and love. With Sheila, he'd been willing to accept "close enough," never expecting to feel what Cindy made so simple. Yet here she was in his arms, and he was willing to do everything humanly possible to keep her there.

Cindy gave a contented sigh. These

few minutes together were as close to paradise as she ever hoped to come in this lifetime. She found it astonishing that they didn't need to speak. The communication between them didn't require words, and when they did talk, they discovered their tastes were surprisingly similar. Cindy loved old movies; so did Thorne. They'd both read everything John LeCarré had ever written and devotedly watched reruns of *Seinfeld*. Both Cindy and Thorne were so familiar with the television comedy that they exchanged lines of dialogue. Excited and happy, they laughed and hugged each other.

Cindy couldn't believe this was happening and held him to her, breathless with an inexplicable joy. Somehow she'd known they'd discover that the night of the Christmas Ball hadn't been a fluke.

Thorne couldn't believe how *right* they were together. They enjoyed the

same things, shared the same interests. He'd never thought he'd find a
woman who could make him laugh
the way Cindy did.

When dinner was ready, Thorne
lit candles, set them in the center of
the dining-room table and dimmed
the overhead lighting. The mood was
wildly romantic.

"The fairy dust is so thick in here I
can barely see," Cindy teased as she
carried their plates to the table.

"That's not fairy dust."

"No?"

"No," he said, and his eyes smiled
into hers. "This is undiluted ro-
mance." He pulled out her chair and
playfully nuzzled her neck when she
was seated.

"I should've recognized what this
is. You'll have to pardon me, but
I've been so busy with school that I
haven't dated much in the past and—"

She stopped abruptly, realizing what she'd said.

Thorne sat down across from her and unfolded the linen napkin. "You go to school?" He'd been so careful not to question her, afraid she'd freeze up if he bombarded her with his need to find answers. From the moment she'd arrived, he'd longed to discover how she'd known he was ill. Cindy was like a complex puzzle. Every bit of information he'd learned about her was a tiny interlocking piece that would help him reveal the complete picture of who and what she was— and why she felt she had to hide from him.

"I attend classes," she admitted, feeling awkward. Without being obvious, she tried to study his reaction, but his face was an unreadable mask. He'd been in business too long to show his feelings.

"What are you studying?"

"Various things." Her stomach fluttered and she sent him a reproving glance before returning her attention to her meal.

Thorne's grip on his fork tightened as he saw her visibly withdraw from him. Her eyes avoiding his, she sat uneasily in the chair; her mouth was pinched as though she was attempting to disguise her pain. Intuitively he knew that if he pressed her for answers, he'd lose her completely. "I won't ask you anything else," he promised.

She smiled then and his heart squeezed with an ufamiliar emotion. The ache caught him by surprise. He didn't care who Cindy was. She could be an escaped convict and it wouldn't matter. He wanted to tell her that regardless of what troubled her, he could fix it. He'd stand between her and the world if that was what it took. Forging rivers, climbing mountains, anything—he'd do it gladly.

After they'd finished eating, Cindy cleared the table. Thorne moved across the living room to change the music.

Blinded by tears, Cindy reached for her coat and purse.

"Do you like classical?" Thorne asked without turning. "How about jazz?"

"Anything is fine." Cindy prayed he didn't hear the quaver in her voice. She shot him one last look, thanking him with her eyes for the second most magnificent night of her life. Then, silently, she slipped out the front door and out of her dreams.

"I've got the music to several Broadway shows if you'd prefer that."

His statement was met with silence. "Cindy?"

He walked into the kitchen. She was gone.

"Cindy?" His voice was hardly audible. He didn't need to look any further. He knew. She'd run away. Vanished into thin air. He found the note propped on the television and read it, then read it again. She asked him to forgive her. He stared at the words coldly.

Thorne folded the paper in half and ripped it viciously, folded it a second time, tore it and crumpled the pieces. His face was rigid and a muscle worked convulsively in his jaw as he threw her note in the garbage. He stood, furious with her, furious with himself for being caught in this trap again.

He slammed his fist against the counter and closed his eyes in an effort to control his anger. Fine, he told himself. If this was how she wanted it, he'd stay out of her life. Thorndike Prince didn't crawl for any woman— they came to him. His face hardened.

He didn't need her; he'd get along perfectly well without her and the silly games she wanted to play. He was more determined than ever to put her out of his mind.

Christmas Day was a nightmare for Cindy. She smiled and responded appropriately to what was going on around her, but she was miserable. She couldn't stop thinking about Thorne. She wondered who he was with and whether he thought of her.... After the sneaky way she'd left him, Cindy believed he probably hated her. She couldn't blame him if he did.

"Cindy, Cindy..." Her four-year-old cousin crawled into her lap. "Will you read to me?"

Carla had always been special to Cindy. The little girl had been born to Cindy's aunt Sofia when she was in her early forties. Sofia's other three children were in their teens and Sofia had been shocked and unhappy about this unexpected pregnancy. But Carla had become the delight of the Territo family.

"Mama's busy and all Tony wants to do is talk to Maria."

"Of course I'll read to you." She hugged Carla tightly.

"You're my favorite cousin," Carla whispered close to Cindy's ear.

"I'm glad, because you're my favorite cousin, too," Cindy whispered back. "Now, do you have a book or do you want me to choose one?"

"Santa brought me a new story."

"Well, good for Santa." Her eye caught Aunt Sofia's and they exchanged knowing glances. The little girl might be only four, but she was well aware that Santa looked just like her dad, Cindy's uncle Carl, after whom Carla had been named.

"I'll get it." Carla scrambled off Cindy's lap, raced across the room and returned with a large picture book. "Here," she said, handing it to Cindy. "Read me this one. Read me *Cinderella*."

Cindy's breath jammed in her lungs and tears stung her eyes. *"Cinderella?"* she repeated as the numbing sensation worked its way through her whole body. She prayed it would anesthetize her from the trauma that gripped her heart.

"Cindy?" Carla's chubby little hands clasped Cindy's knee. "Aren't you going to read to me?"

"Of course, sweetheart." Somehow she managed to pick up the book and flip open the front cover. Carla positioned herself comfortably in her cousin's lap, leaned back and promptly inserted her thumb in her mouth.

It took all of Cindy's energy to start reading. Her throat felt incredibly dry. "'Once upon a time...'"

* * *

"...in a land far, far away," Mary Susan Clark told her five-year-old son, who sat on the brocade cushion at her feet.

Thorne gazed at his sister, who was reciting the fairy tale to her son, and his heart slowed with anger and resentment. "Do you think it's a good idea to be filling a young boy's head with that kind of garbage?" Thorne demanded gruffly.

Mary Susan's gray eyes widened with surprise. "But it's only a fairy tale."

"Thorne." His mother studied him, her expression puzzled. "It's not like you to snap."

"I apologize," he said with a weak smile. "I guess I've been a bit short-tempered lately."

"You've been ill." Sheila, with her dark brown eyes and pixie face, automatically defended him. She placed her hand in his and gave his fingers a gentle squeeze.

He liked Sheila well enough; she was unfailingly pleasant and loyal. One day she'd make some man an excellent wife. Maybe even him. Thorne was through playing Cindy's games. Through believing in fairy tales. He couldn't live like this. Cindy didn't want anything to do with him, and he had no choice but to accept her wishes. Sheila loved him—at least she claimed she did. Thorne didn't know what love felt like anymore. At one time he'd thought he was in love with Sheila. Maybe not *completely,* but he'd expected that to happen eventually. Then he'd met Cindy, and he was head over heels in love for the first time in his thirty-three years. Crazy in love. And with a woman who'd turned her back on him and walked away without a second thought. It didn't make sense. Nothing did anymore. Nothing at all. Not business. Not life. Not women.

Thorne and Sheila had been seeing each other for nearly six months and she'd hardly been able to conceal her disappointment when an engagement ring hadn't been secretly tucked under the Christmas tree. But she hadn't questioned him. He wished she wasn't so understanding; he would've preferred it if she'd gotten angry, demanded an explanation.

Thorne noticed his mother still studying him and he made an attempt to disguise his unhappiness. Smiling required a monumental effort. He managed it, but he doubted he'd fooled his mother.

"Thorne, could you help me in the kitchen?"

The whole family turned to him. That was code for talking privately, and it wasn't the least bit original.

"Of course, Mother," he said with

the faintest sardonic inflection. He disentangled his fingers from Sheila's and stood, obediently following Gwendolyn Prince out of the room.

"What in heaven's name is the matter with you?" she snapped the minute they were out of earshot. "It isn't that…that girl you mentioned, is it?"

"What girl?" Feigning ignorance seemed the best response.

"You haven't been yourself…"

"…since the night of that Christmas Ball," Aunt Theresa said softly.

"I know," Cindy whispered. "You see, there's something I didn't realize…. Fairy tales don't always come true."

"But, Cindy, you're so unhappy over him."

"We said goodbye," she said, her eyes pleading with her aunt to drop this disturbing subject. Accepting that she'd live without Thorne was difficult enough; discussing it with her aunt was like tearing open a half-healed wound.

"You haven't stopped thinking about him."

"No, but I will."

"Will you, Cindy?" Theresa's deep brown eyes showed her doubt.

Cindy's gaze pleaded with her. "Yes," she said and the words were a vow to herself. She had no choice now. When she'd left Thorne's apartment it had been forever. Although the pain had been nearly unbearable, it was better to sever the ties quickly than to bleed slowly to death.

"Mother and I are planning a shopping expedition to Paris in March," Sheila said enthusiastically, sitting across the table from Thorne.

They were at one of Thorne's favorite lunch spots. Sheila made it a habit to visit the office at least once a week so they could have lunch. In the past, Thorne had looked forward to their get-togethers. Not today. He wasn't in the mood. But before he'd been able to say anything to Ms. Hillard, she'd sent Sheila into his office, and now he was stuck.

"Paris sounds interesting."

"So does the chicken," Sheila commented, glancing over the menu. "I hear the mushroom sauce here is fabulous."

Thorne's stomach turned. "Baked chicken breast served with mushroom sauce," he read, remembering all too well his last evening with Cindy and the meal she'd prepared for him.

"I hope you'll try it with me," Sheila urged, gazing at him adoringly.

His mouth thinned. "I hate mushrooms."

Sheila stared down at the menu and she pressed her lips tightly together.

"I didn't know that," she said after a long moment.

"You do now," Thorne muttered, detesting himself for treating her this way. Sheila deserved better.

The waiter came to the table, hands behind his back. "Are you ready to order?"

"I believe so," Thorne said, closing his menu and handing it back. "The lady will have the chicken special and I'll have a mushroom omelet."

Sheila gave him an odd look, but said nothing.

During lunch Thorne made a sincere effort to be pleasant. He honestly tried to appear interested when Sheila told him about the latest fashion trends in France. He even managed to stifle a yawn when she hinted at the possibility of buying several yards of exclusive French lace. It wasn't until they'd left the restaurant and were walking toward his office that Thorne understood the implication. French lace—wedding gown.

Suddenly something caught his attention.

There. The blonde, half a block ahead of him. *Cindy.* It was Cindy.

"And I was thinking…"

Sheila's voice faded and Thorne quickened his pace.

"Thorne," Sheila said breathlessly. "You're walking so fast I can't keep up with you."

Without thought, he removed her hand from his arm. "Excuse me a minute." He didn't take his eyes off Cindy, fearing he'd lose her in the heavy holiday crowds.

"Thorne?"

He ignored Sheila and took off running, weaving in and around the people filling the sidewalk on Sixth Avenue.

"Cindy!" He yelled her name, but either she didn't hear or she was trying to escape him. Again. He wouldn't let her. He'd found her now. Relief flowed through him and he savored the sweet taste of it. He'd dreamed this would happen. Somehow, some way, he'd miraculously stumble upon her. Every time he stepped outside, he found himself studying faces, looking. Searching for her in a silent quest that dominated his every waking thought. And now she was only a few feet away, her brisk pace no match for his easy sprint. Her shoulder-length blond hair swayed back and forth, and her navy wool coat was wrapped securely around her.

Thorne raced around two couples, cutting abruptly in front of them. He didn't know what he'd do first—kiss her or shake her. Kiss her, he decided.

"Cindy." He finally caught up with her and put his hand on her shoulder.

"I beg your pardon." The woman, maybe fifty, slapped his hand away.

She didn't even resemble Cindy. She was older, plain, and embarrassed by his attention.

Thorne blinked back the disbelief. "I thought you were someone else."

"Obviously. Mind your manners, young man, or I'll report you to the police."

"I apologize." He couldn't move. His feet felt rooted to the sidewalk and his arms hung lifelessly at his sides. Cindy was driving him mad; he was slowly but surely losing his sanity.

"Decent women aren't safe in this city anymore," the woman grumbled and quickly stepped away.

"Thorne! Thorne!" Sheila joined him, her hands gripping his arm. "Who was she?"

"No one." He couldn't stop looking at the blonde as she made her way down the street. He would've sworn it was Cindy. He would've wagered a year's salary that the woman who couldn't escape him fast enough had been Cindy. His Cindy. His love.

"Thorne," Sheila droned, patting his hand. "You've been working too hard. I'm worried about you."

"I'm fine," he said absently.

The pinched look returned to Sheila's face, but she didn't argue. "March gives you plenty of time to arrange a vacation. We'll enjoy Paris. I'll take you shopping with me and let you pick out my trousseau."

"I'm not going to Paris," he snapped.

Sheila continued to pat his hand. "I do wish you'd consider it. You haven't been yourself, Thorne. Not at all."

He couldn't agree more.

Two hours later Thorne sat at his desk reading financial statements the accounting department had sent up for him to approve.

"Mr. Williams is here," Ms. Hillard informed him.

Thorne closed the folder. "Send him in."

"Right away," Ms. Hillard returned crisply.

Thorne stood to greet the balding man who wore a suit that looked as if it hadn't been dry-cleaned since it came off the rack at Sears ten years before. His potbelly gave credence to his reputation as the best private detective in the business; from the looks of it, he ate well enough.

"Mr. Williams," Thorne said, extending his hand to the other man.

"Call me Mike."

They exchanged brisk handshakes. The man's grip was solid. Thorne approved.

"What can I do for you?" Mike asked as he sat down.

"I want you to find someone for me," Thorne said, without preamble.

Mike nodded. "It's what I do. What's the name?"

Thorne reclaimed his chair and his hands clutched the armrest as he leaned back, giving an impression of indifference. This wasn't going to be easy. "Cindy."

"Last name?" The detective reached for his pencil and pad.

"I don't know." He paused. "I'm not actually sure Cindy's her first name. It could've been made up." Thorne was braced to accept anything where Cindy was concerned. Everything and anything.

"Where did you meet her?"

"At a party. The one put on by this company. She doesn't work here. I've already checked."

Williams nodded.

"She did leave this behind." Thorne leaned forward to hand the detective the comb. It was missing one pearl, he saw to his dismay. "I've had it appraised and the comb isn't uncommon. She has two, and she claims they belonged to her mother. There are no markings that would distinguish this one from ten thousand other identical combs."

Again Williams nodded, but he examined the comb carefully. "Can I take this?" he asked and stuck it in his pocket.

Thorne agreed with a swift nod of his head. "I'll want it back."

"Of course."

They spoke for an additional fifteen minutes and Thorne recalled with as much clarity as possible each of the two meetings he'd had with Cindy.

Williams stopped him only once. "A limo, you said."

"Yes." Thorne slid forward in his chair. He'd forgotten that. Cindy had gotten into a limousine that first night when she'd escaped from him. She'd handed him his coat, run across the street and been met by a long black limousine.

"You wouldn't happen to remember the license plate, would you?"

"No." Thorne shook his head disgustedly. "I'm afraid I can't."

"Don't worry about it. I have enough." Williams scanned the details he'd listed and flipped the pad shut. He got to his feet.

Thorne stood, too. "Can you find her?" he asked.

"I'll give it my best shot."

"Good." Thorne hoped the man couldn't see how desperate he'd become.

A cold northern wind chilled Cindy's arms as she waited on the sidewalk outside the Oakes-Jenning building. It was well past midnight. She was exhausted—physically and mentally. She hadn't been sleeping well and the paper she should be writing during the holiday break just wouldn't come, although she'd done all the research. It was because of Thorne. No matter what she did, she couldn't stop thinking about him.

Uncle Sal pulled to a stop at the curb. Cindy stepped away from the building and climbed into the front seat beside him.

"Hi," she said, forcing a smile. Her family was worried about her and Cindy did her best to ease their fears.

"A private detective was poking around the house today," her uncle announced, starting into the traffic.

Cindy felt her heart go cold. "What did he want?"

"He was asking about you."

Seven

"Asking about me… What did you tell him?"

"Not a thing."

"But…"

"He wanted to look at my appointment schedule for December 12, but I wouldn't let him."

The chilly sensation that had settled over Cindy dropped below freezing. Her uncle's refusal would only create suspicion. The detective would be back, and there'd be more questions Sal would refuse to answer. The detective wouldn't accept that, and he'd return again and again until he had the information he wanted. This stranger would make trouble for her family. In a hundred years, she never would've guessed that Thorne would go to such lengths to locate her. She had to find a way to stop him...a way to make him understand and leave things as they were.

Cindy went to bed still thinking about the whole mess and got up even more tired and troubled than she'd been before. She'd repeatedly examined her own role in this situation. Playing the part of Cinderella for one night had seemed so innocent, so adventurous, so exciting. She'd slipped into the fantasy with ease, but the night had ended with the stroke of midnight and she could never go back to being a fairy-tale character again. She'd let go of the illusion and yes, it had been painful, but she'd had no choice. The consequences of that one foolhardy night would follow her for the rest of her life.

She'd never dreamed it would be possible to feel as strongly about a man in so short a time as she did about Thorne. But her emotion wasn't based on any of the usual prerequisites for love. It couldn't be. They'd only seen each other twice.

Thorne might believe he felt as strongly about her, Cindy realized, but that wasn't real either. She was a challenge—the mystery woman who'd briefly touched his life. Once he learned the truth and recognized that she'd made a fool of him, it would be over. Given no alternative, Cindy knew she'd have to tell Thorne who she really was.

"He could get me fired," she said aloud several soul-searching hours later. Her hands clutched her purse protectively as she waited outside the Oakes-Jenning Financial Services building. Employees streamed out in a steady flow. Cindy stood against the side of the building, just far enough back to examine their faces as they made their way out. They all looked so serious. Cindy didn't know much about the business world, but it certainly seemed to employ dour people, Thorne included.

For most of the afternoon, Cindy had weighed the possible consequences of telling Thorne the truth. Losing her job was only one of several unpleasant options that had entered her mind. And ultimately he could hate her, which would be so much worse than anything else he could do. She wanted to scream at him for being so obstinate, so willful, so determined to be part of her life. He had to know she didn't want to be found, and yet he'd ignored her wishes and driven her to this. He'd forced her into doing the one thing she dreaded most—telling him the truth.

Her tenacity hardened as she watched Thorne step out of the building, his face as sober as everyone else's. He carried a briefcase in one hand and walked briskly past her. Unseeing. Uncaring. As oblivious to her then as he was every morning when he walked into his clean office.

"Thorne." She didn't shout; her voice was little more than a whisper.

He stopped abruptly, almost in midstride, and turned around. "Cindy?" His gaze scanned the sea of faces that swam before him. "Cindy?" he repeated, louder this time, unsure if this was real. He'd been half out of his mind for days on end. Nothing shocked him anymore. He'd known her voice instantly, but that too could be part of his deep yearning to find her. She was here and she'd called out to him, and he wouldn't let her escape him again.

"Here." She took a step closer, her hands clenched in fists at her sides. "Call off the detective. I'll tell you—" She wasn't allowed to finish.

Thorne dropped the briefcase onto the sidewalk, grabbed her shoulders and hauled her into his arms. His mouth came down on hers with such intensity that he drove the breath from her lungs. His hand dug into her hair as he tangled it with his fingers, as though binding her to him. His mouth on hers left her in no doubt regarding the strength of his emotions.

Cindy's first reaction was stunned surprise. She'd expected him to be furious, to shout at her and demand an explanation. But not this. Never this.

Once the initial shock of his kiss faded, she surrendered to the sheer pleasure of simply being in his arms. She held on to him, throwing her arms around him, relishing the rush of sensations that sprang up within her. She couldn't have pushed him away had her life depended on it. The resolution to end their relationship had melted the minute he'd touched her.

"This had better not be a dream," Thorne said, moving his lips against her temple. "You taste so unbelievably real."

Cindy flattened her palms against his chest in an attempt to break away, but he held on to her. "Thorne, please, people are looking."

"Let them." He kissed her again, with such hunger that she was left breathless and disoriented. She made a weak effort to break loose again.

"Thorne," she pleaded. Every second he continued to hold her weakened her determination to explain everything. He felt so warm and vital…so wonderful. "Please…don't," she begged as he covered her face with kisses. Even as she spoke, pleading with him to stop, she was turning her head one way and then another, allowing him to do as he wished.

"I'm starving for you," he murmured, kissing her again.

She was so weak-willed with Thorne. She could start out with the firmest of resolves but after being with him for ten seconds she had no fortitude left at all.

"Cindy—" his arms tightened "—I've been going crazy without you."

It hadn't been any less traumatic for Cindy. "You hired a detective?"

"He found you?"

"No...I heard you were looking." Her hands lovingly framed his face. "Thorne, please call him off." She didn't want the private detective harassing or intimidating those she loved most. "I'll tell you everything you want to know...only, please, please, don't hate me."

"Hate you?" His look was incredulous. "I'm not capable of feeling any different toward you than the night we met." For the first time he seemed to notice the stares they were generating. "Let's get out of here." He reached for her hand and led her purposefully away.

"Thorne," she cried with a surprised glance over her shoulder. "Your briefcase."

He seemed so utterly astonished that he could have forgotten it, Cindy laughed outright.

Without hesitating, he turned and went back to retrieve it, dragging her with him. "See what you do to me?" His words were distressed.

"Do you know what you do to me?" she responded with equal consternation.

"I must have quite an effect on you,

all right. You can't seem to get away from me fast enough. You sneak off like a thief in the night and turn up when I least expect it. I don't sleep well, my appetite's gone and I'm convinced you're playing me for a fool."

"Oh, Thorne, you don't honestly believe that, do you?" She came to an abrupt stop. People had to walk around them, but Cindy didn't care. She couldn't bear it if Thorne believed anything less than what she truly felt for him. "I think I'd rather die than let you assume for even a minute that I didn't care for you."

"You have one heck of a way of showing it."

"But, Thorne, if you'd give me a chance to—"

Undaunted by the traffic, Thorne paraded them halfway into the street, his arm raised. "Taxi!"

"Where are we going?"

A Yellow cab pulled up in front of

them. Thorne ignored her question; he opened the car door and climbed in beside her a second later.

Before Cindy could say another word, Thorne spoke to the driver. When he'd finished he leaned back and stared at her as though he still wasn't completely sure she was really there.

Cindy hadn't thought about *where* she'd talk to Thorne, only that she would. Over and over she'd rehearsed what she wanted to say. But she hadn't counted on him hauling her across Manhattan to some unknown destination. From the looks he was giving her now, he didn't appear any too pleased with her.

Thorne finally relaxed and expelled a long sigh. "Do you realize we've been to bed together and I don't even know your name?"

Cindy felt more than saw the driver's interest perk up. Color exploded into her cheeks as she glared hotly at Thorne. "Would you stop it?" she hissed. He was doing this on purpose, to punish her.

"I don't think I can." He regarded her levelly. "You've got me so twisted up inside, I don't know what's real and what's not anymore. My parents think I need to see a shrink and I'm beginning to agree with them!"

Cindy covered his hand with her own. "I'm certainly nothing like the Cinderella you met that night." Her voice was a raw whisper, filled with pain. "I thought I could pretend to be something I'm not for one glamorous night, but it all backfired. I've hated deceiving you—you deserve better than me."

"Is your name really Cindy?"

She nodded. "That's what started it all. Now I wish I'd been named Hermione or Frieda—anything but Cindy. If I had, then maybe I wouldn't have believed in that night and decided to do something so stupid."

"No matter who you are and what you've done," Thorne told her solemnly, "I'll never regret the Christmas Ball."

"That's the problem—I can't either. I'll treasure it always. But Thorne, don't you see? I'm *not* Cinderella. I'm only me."

"In case you haven't noticed, I'm not exactly Prince Charming."

"But you are," Cindy argued.

"No. And that's been our problem all along—we each seemed to think the other wanted to continue the fantasy." He put his arm around her and drew her close to his side. "That evening was marvelous, but it was one night in a million. If we're going to develop a relationship, it has to be between the people we are now."

Cindy leaned against him, sighed

inwardly and closed her eyes as he rested his chin on her head.

"I want to be with Cindy," he said tenderly, "not the imaginary Cinderella."

"But Cindy will disappoint you."

"If you're looking for Prince Charming in me, then you're in for a sad awakening as well."

"You don't even know who I am!"

"It doesn't matter." Her lovely face commanded all his attention. He sensed that something deep inside her was insecure and frightened. She'd bolted and run away from him twice, her doubts overtaking her. No more. Whatever Williams had dug up about her had brought her back. She was here because Mike had gotten close to her, had begun to uncover her secrets.

Thorne had found his Cindy again and could on go with his life. The restless feeling that had worn away at him was dissipating. He was a man who liked his privacy, but overnight he'd discovered he was lonely and could no longer adjust to the solitude. Not when he'd met the one woman he wanted to share his world with. All he had to do was persuade *her* of that. Only this time, he'd be more cautious. He wouldn't make demands of her. She could tell him whatever was troubling her when she was ready. Every time he started questioning her, it ended in disaster.

Cindy sat upright, her back stiff as she turned her head and glanced out the side window. She knew he was right; they couldn't go back to the night of the Christmas Ball. But she wasn't completely convinced they could form a lasting relationship as Thorne and Cindy.

"You say it doesn't matter," she said thoughtfully, "but when I tell you I'm the girl who—"

"Stop." His hand reached for hers,

squeezing her fingers tightly. "Are you married, engaged or currently involved with another man?"

She glared at him for even suggesting such a thing. "No, of course not!"

"Involved in any illegal activity?"

She moved several inches away from him and sat starchly erect, shocked at his questions. "Is *that* what you think?"

"Just answer me."

"No!" She had difficulty saying it. She tucked a strand of hair behind her ear in nervous agitation. "I don't cheat, rarely lie and am thoroughly law-abiding—I don't even jaywalk, and in New York that's something!"

Thorne's warm smile chased the chill from her bones. "Then, who and what you are is of no importance. You're the one who has all the objections. What I feel is apparently of little consequence to you."

"That's not true. I'm only trying to save you from embarrassment."

"Embarrassment?"

"My family name isn't linked with three generations of banking."

"I wouldn't care if it was linked with generations of garbage collecting."

"You say that now," she snapped.

"I mean that. I'm falling in love with a girl named Cindy, not a fairy-tale figure who magically appeared in my life. She's bright and funny and loving."

Falling in love with her! Cindy's heart felt like it was going to burst with happiness. Then she realized—once again—the impossibility of an enduring relationship between them. Dejectedly she lowered her gaze. "Please don't say that."

"What? That I'm falling in love with you?"

"Yes."

"It's true."

"But you hardly know me," she said. Yet that hadn't deterred *her* from falling head over heels for him.

The taxi came to a stop in the heavy traffic, and the driver told them, "Central Park is on your left."

"Central Park?" Cindy echoed, pleased at his choice of locations to do their talking. She hadn't paid attention to where they were going.

"I thought we should return here and start over again."

She got out as Thorne paid the driver. A moment later, he joined Cindy on the sidewalk. He placed her hand in the crook of his arm and smiled seductively down on her.

Her returning smile was feeble at best.

"Hello, there," he said softly. "I'm Thorne, which is short for Thorndike, which was my father's name and his father's before him."

"I'm a first-generation Cindy."

"Well, Cindy, now that we've been properly introduced, will you have dinner with me tonight?"

"I…can't." She hated to refuse, but she couldn't spend time with him when she was paid to clean his office. As it was, she was due there within half an hour.

His face tightened briefly. "Can't or won't?"

"Can't."

"Tomorrow, then."

"But it's New Year's Eve." Surely he had other places to go and more important people to spend the evening with. Arguments clustered in her mind and were dispelled with one enticing look from Thorne.

"New Year's Eve or not, I'll pick you up and we'll paint the town." He felt Cindy tense and guessed why. Quickly he amended his suggestion.

"I'll meet you somewhere. Anyplace you say."

"In front of Oakes-Jenning." Although it was a holiday, she'd be working; she couldn't afford to turn down time and a half. "I...won't be available until after eleven-thirty."

"Fine, I'll be there."

"You're late," Vanessa said unnecessarily when Cindy ran breathlessly into the basement supply room.

"I know."

"Where were you?"

"Central Park." She made busy work filling her cart with the needed supplies. She'd left after promising Thorne she'd meet him the following night. His gaze had pleaded with her to give him something to hold on to—a phone number, a name, anything. But Cindy had given him something of far greater value—her word. Letting her go had been a measure of his trust. She could see that he wasn't pleased, but he hadn't drilled her with questions or made any other demands.

What he'd said was true. Neither of them could continue playing the role of someone they weren't. Cinderella was now Cindy and Prince Charming had gone back to being Thorne. They'd been a bit awkward with each other at first, but gradually that unease had evaporated.

Cindy was beginning to believe that although there were many obstacles blocking their path, together they might be able to overcome them. There hadn't been time to say the things she needed to say because she'd had to rush to work. She hadn't explained that to Thorne and saw jealousy appear on his face.

"What are you thinking?" Vanessa asked, studying her.

"Nothing."

"Nothing?" her friend complained. "Give me a break! Are we back to that?"

Cindy relented. "I'm seeing Thorne tomorrow night."

"You are?" Even Vanessa sounded shocked. "But it's New Year's Eve... oh, heavens, did you forget we have to work?"

"No...I told him I wouldn't be ready until after eleven-thirty."

"And he didn't ask for any explanation?"

"Not really." The questions had been there, in his eyes, but he hadn't voiced a single one. Cindy felt her friend regarding her thoughtfully and busied herself with the cart, making sure she had everything she needed before heading for the upper floor.

She only hoped she was doing the right thing. Thorne kept insisting that who she was didn't matter to him. She

was going to test that and in the process wager her heart and her future
happiness.

"Thorne, I've been trying to reach
you."
Thorne frowned at the telephone
receiver. He could tell by the slight
edge to his mother's voice that she
was going to bring up an unpleasant
subject—Sheila. The other woman
was quickly becoming a thorn in his
side. No pun intended.
"Yes, Mother," he returned obediently, throwing his magazine on the
coffee table. This conversation would
require his full attention.
"Your father and I are having a New
Year's Eve party tomorrow night and
we'd like you to attend."
He'd never enjoyed parties, which
was one reason his mother had been
so keen on Sheila, who loved to so-
cialize. Sheila would be good for his

career, his father had once told him. At the time, Thorne had considered that an important factor in choosing a wife. Not anymore.

"I apologize, Mother, but I'll have to decline, I've already made plans."

"But Sheila said—"

"I won't be with Sheila," he responded shortly.

"Oh, dear, is it that Cheryl woman again? I'd thought that was over."

"Cindy," he corrected, swallowing a laugh. He knew his mother—she remembered Cindy's name as well as she did her own.

"I see," his mother said, her voice sharpening with disapproval. "Then you haven't said anything to Sheila."

"As I recall, you advised me against it," he reminded her.

"But, Thorne, the dear girl is beside herself with worry. And what's this about you chasing a strange woman down some sidewalk? Really, Thorne, what's gotten into you?"

"I'm in love."

The horrified silence that followed his announcement nearly made him laugh into the phone. His parents had been waiting years for him to announce that he'd chosen a wife, and now that he was in love, they acted as if he'd committed a terrible crime. However, Thorne was positive that once his parents met Cindy, they'd understand, and love her, too.

"Are you claiming to love a woman you hardly know?"

"That's right, Mother."

"What about her family?"

"What about them?"

"Thorne!"

His mother sounded aghast, which only increased Thorne's amusement. "Would you feel better if you could meet her?"

"I'm not sure...I suppose it would help."

"Dinner, then, the first part of next week. I'll clear it with Cindy and get back to you."

"Fine." But she didn't seem enthusiastic. "In the meantime, would you talk to Sheila? She hasn't heard from you all week."

"What do you suggest I say to her?"

"Tell her...tell her you need a few days to think things over. That should appease her for now. Once I've had a chance to...meet your Cheryl, I'll have a better sense of the situation."

"Yes, Mother," he said obediently and replaced the receiver. Family had always been important to Thorne, but he wouldn't allow his mother or anyone else to rule his life.

Leaning back, Thorne folded his arms behind his head. He felt good, wonderful. He'd never looked forward to anything more than tomorrow night. New Year's Eve with Cindy. And with it, the promise of spending every year together for the rest of his life.

The following day, Thorne worked until noon. He did some errands, ate a light dinner around six, showered and dressed casually. The television killed several hours, but he found himself glancing at his watch every few minutes. He'd leave around eleven, he figured. That would give him plenty of time to get to Oakes-Jenning, and from there he'd take Cindy to Times Square. It was something he'd always wanted to do, but had never had the chance. They could lose themselves in the crowd and he'd have every excuse to keep her close.

The doorbell chimed around eight, and Thorne hurried to answer, convinced it was Cindy. Somehow, some way, she'd come to him early. His excitement died when he saw Sheila standing in the hallway.

"Sheila."

"Hello, Thorne." She peered up at him through seductively thick lashes. "May I come in?"

He stepped aside. "Sure."

"You're looking very casual." She entered the apartment, removed her coat and sat on the sofa. Wearing a slinky, low-cut black dress, she looked anything *but* casual.

"This is a surprise." He stood awkwardly in the center of the room, hands buried in his pockets.

"I haven't heard from you since our luncheon date and thought I'd stop in unannounced. I hope you don't mind?"

Thorne would have preferred her to choose another day, but since she'd come, he might as well use the opportunity to tell her about Cindy. "I'm glad you did." At the happiness that flashed in her eyes, Thorne regretted his poor choice of words.

She folded her hands in her lap and regarded him with such adoration that Thorne felt his stomach knot.

"Sometimes I do such a terrible job of explaining my feelings," she said softly, lowering her gaze to her hands. "I want you to know how much you mean to me."

The knot in Thorne's stomach worked its way up to his chest. "I treasure your friendship, as well."

She arched her brows. "I thought we were more than simply friends. Much more."

Thorne sat on the ottoman and rolled it toward Sheila so that he sat directly in front of her. "This isn't easy."

"Don't." She shook her head. "I already know what you're going to say.... You've met someone else."

"I don't want to hurt you." They'd

been seeing each other steadily for months, and although he'd come to realize how mismatched they were, Sheila hadn't seen it yet, and he honestly wished to spare her any pain.

"But, darling, you don't need to. I understand about these things."

"You do?" Thorne hadn't the foggiest notion what there was for her to understand.

"A woman has to accept this sort of thing from her husband. I know Daddy's had his women on the side. Mother's aware of it, too."

Thorne surged to his feet. "You're saying you expect me to have an *affair?*"

"Just to get her out of your system. I want you to know I understand."

Years of discipline tempered Thorne's response. He was so furious that it took all his restraint to continue being civil after Sheila's announcement. He marched to the plate-glass window and looked out, afraid to speak for fear of what he'd say. Instead he analyzed his anger.

"Thorne, you look upset."

"I am." He realized he was so outraged because Sheila's seeming generosity had insulted Cindy by suggesting she belonged on some back street.

"But why?"

"Cindy isn't that kind of woman," he said, and turned around. "And neither are you."

A gush of feminine tears followed. Embarrassed, Thorne retrieved a box of tissues and held Sheila gently in his arms until she'd finished weeping.

Dabbing her eyes, Sheila said she needed something to drink and nodded approvingly when Thorne brought out a bottle of expensive French wine he knew she liked. He had plenty of time to soothe her wounded ego.

Cindy wouldn't be available until almost midnight.

Once Sheila had dried her eyes, she was good company, chatting about the fun times they'd shared over the months they'd been seeing each other and getting slightly tipsy in the process.

Slowly, Thorne felt his anger evaporate. Sheila did most of the talking, and when she suggested they have a cocktail at the Carlyle, Thorne agreed. It was still two hours before he could meet Cindy.

The Carlyle was crowded, as were two of Sheila's other favorite hangouts where they stopped for drinks.

"Let's drop in at your parents'," she said casually, swirling the ice in her empty glass.

"I can't. I'm meeting Cindy." He raised his arm to look at his watch and the air left his lungs in one disbelieving gasp. "I'm late."

"But, Thorne…"

It was already eleven forty-five and he was at least another fifteen minutes from Oakes-Jenning. And his cell phone was useless—he had no number for her, no surname, nothing. The regret seared through him.

"You can't just leave me here!" Sheila cried, trotting after him.

He handed their ticket to the coat-check girl and paced restlessly until she returned. When she did, Thorne thrust her a generous tip.

"Thorne." Sheila gave him a forlorn look, her eyes damp with tears. "Don't leave me."

Eight

All of New York seemed alive with activity to Cindy. New Year's Eve, and it could've been noon for all the people milling in the streets. Times Square would be a madhouse, filled with anxious spectators waiting for the magical hour when the New Year's Eve ball would descend, marking the beginning of another year.

Cindy felt wonderful. Free. Thorne might have claimed not to be Prince Charming, but he'd demonstrated some truly princely qualities. Judging by the way he'd searched for her, he seemed to feel genuine affection. Surely he wouldn't have hired a private detective to find her if he didn't care. Nor would he have been willing to overlook the secrecy she wore like a heavy shroud. He didn't like it, but he accepted it. He claimed it didn't matter who or what she was, and to prove his point he'd refused to listen when she'd tried to explain. He didn't insist on answers even though the questions were clearly written in his eyes, nor did he make unreasonable demands. She'd told him she couldn't meet him until eleven-thirty, and without voicing any qualms he'd agreed to that.

A police car, with its siren screaming, raced down the street and Cindy watched its progress. A glance at her watch told her Thorne was fifteen minutes late. After months of cleaning his office, Cindy could confidently say that he was rarely late for anything. He was too much of a businessman to be unaware of the clock.

Remembering the police car, Cindy stepped to the curb and looked up and down the street. Unexpectedly, she felt alarmed. Perhaps something had happened to Thorne. Perhaps he was lying somewhere hurt and bleeding— or maybe he'd suffered a relapse and was ill again.

Cindy couldn't bear to think of him in pain. She'd rather endure it herself than have him suffer. It took her another five minutes to reason things out. Thorne was perfectly capable of looking after himself, and she was worrying needlessly. He'd gotten tied up in traffic and would arrive any minute. If he was hurt, she told herself, she'd know. Somehow, her heart would know. Thorne would come to her, regardless of the circumstances. All she had to do was be patient and wait. He couldn't look at her the way he did and ask her to spend this special night with him and then leave her standing in the cold. She'd stake her life on it.

Thirty minutes later, Cindy's confidence was dying a slow, painful death. She was cold. Her face felt frozen and her toes were numb. She'd been silly enough to wear open-toed pumps and was paying the price of her own folly. She hunched her shoulders against the wind that whipped her hair back and forth across her face. Resentfully she thought of how hard she'd worked, rushing from one office to another to finish early, and how quickly she'd showered and changed clothes—all so she could spend extra time on her hair and makeup. She'd wanted this night to be perfect for Thorne. But after forty-five minutes of standing in the wind, her hair was a lost cause and her makeup couldn't have fared any better.

Another fifteen minutes, Cindy decided. That was all she'd give him.

And then fifteen intolerable, interminable minutes passed.

Five more, she vowed, and that was it. She'd walk away. Thorne would have a logical explanation, she was sure of it, but she couldn't stand in the cold all night.

Dejected and discouraged, Cindy waited out the allotted five minutes and decided there was nothing she could do but leave. Drawing her coat more tightly around her, she walked to the corner and paused. Not yet. She couldn't leave yet. What if Thorne arrived and they just missed each other? She couldn't bear for him to find her gone. He'd be frantic. Even if she'd had a cell phone, she wouldn't have known how to reach him.

She pulled her hand from her pocket and studied her watch one last time. Maybe she should wait another minute or two—it wouldn't hurt. Her toes were beyond feeling and a few more minutes wouldn't matter.

A niggling voice in the back of her mind tried to convince her that Thorne had left her waiting in the cold as punishment for disrupting his staid, regimented life.

Forcefully, Cindy shook her head. She refused to believe it. The voice returned a moment later, suggesting that he was with another woman. Sheila. This possibility seemed far more feasible. Sheila's photograph remained on prominent display in his office. A hundred doubts crowded each other in her troubled thoughts. Sheila. He was with Sheila!

Determined now to leave, Cindy buried her hands deeper in the pockets of her wool coat. It was too late to ring in the New Year with Thorne. Too late to believe that a relationship between them could work. Too late to demand her heart back!

Hunched against the piercing wind, her collar as close to her face as she could arrange it, Cindy turned and walked away.

The sound of tires screeching to a halt and a car door slamming startled her.

"Cindy!"

She turned to find Thorne racing toward her.

Breathless, he caught her in his arms and held her to him. He pushed the hair from her face as though he needed to read her expression and see for himself that she was safe and secure. "Oh, Cindy, I'm sorry, so sorry."

Every wild suspicion died the minute Thorne reached for her. He was so warm and he held her as though he planned to do it for a good long while. "You came," she murmured, laughing with pure relief. "You came." She slid her arms around his middle and tucked her head beneath his chin. She noticed there was something different about his usually distinctive masculine scent, as if it were mingled with some other fragrance.... But she was too deliriously happy at being in his arms to puzzle it out right now.

"You must be half-frozen," Thorne moaned, nuzzling her hair.

"Three-quarters," she joked. "But it was worth every second just to be with you now."

He kissed her then, his mouth cherishing hers. Cindy absorbed his warmth, focusing on him like a flower turning toward the sun, seeking its nourishing rays as the source of all life.

Thorne lifted his head, cradled her chilled face in both hands and released a sigh that came from deep within him. He'd been overwrought, checking his watch every ten seconds, half crazed with fear that she'd walk out of his life and he'd never find her again. The traffic had been a nightmare, the streets crammed with cars and people. He hadn't dreamed she'd still be there waiting, although he prayed she was. An *hour* she'd stood and waited in the freezing cold. He cursed Sheila and then himself.

"Let's get out of here," he said breathlessly. Slipping his arm around her waist, he led her back to the taxi and helped her inside. He paused long enough to ask the driver to take them to a nearby restaurant.

Inside the cab, Cindy removed her shoes and started to rub feeling back into her numb toes.

"Let me do that," Thorne insisted, holding her nylon-covered feet between his large hands and rubbing vigorously.

Cindy sighed, relaxed and leaned against the back of the seat.

"Better?"

She nodded, content just to be with Thorne. "Where are we going?"

"Someplace where I can get some Irish coffee into you."

"I'm Italian," she said with a smile.

"Italian?" He eyed her curiously. "But you're blond."

"There are plenty of us, trust me."

They arrived at the restaurant, but it wasn't one that Cindy recognized. Thorne helped her climb out of the taxi, then paid the driver and escorted her inside the lounge. They were given a table immediately, although the place was crowded. Cindy realized the large bill Thorne passed the maître d' had something to do with the waiting table.

Once they were seated, Thorne expelled his breath in a deep sigh. "I feel like I've been running a marathon," he said.

"What happened?"

The waitress arrived and Thorne ordered their drinks, glad of the interruption. He was going to lie to Cindy. It was only a lie of omission, but it bothered him. He expected her to be honest, and it felt wrong to be less so with her. "I miscalculated the time and got caught in traffic. I didn't dare hope you'd still be there. I don't know what I would've done if you'd left."

"I'd already decided to contact you in the morning."

He closed his eyes. "Thank God for that."

"You wanted to give us—the unprincely Thorne and the unadorned Cinderella—a chance, and I agreed, didn't I?"

"Yes."

He looked at her, his eyes tender and loving. "We didn't ring in the New Year together." His words revealed his regret.

"I know." She dropped her gaze because looking at him was too intense, like staring into the sun for too long. She was becoming blind to the facts that surrounded their unusual relationship, ignoring the overwhelming potential for emotional pain.

The waitress brought their drinks and Cindy sipped the liquor-laced coffee. It was hot, sweet and potent, instantly spreading its warmth. The tingling sensation left her toes and fingers almost immediately.

"Next year we'll make it to Times Square?" Thorne suggested, his voice lifting slightly at the end of the statement.

"Next year," she agreed, desperately wanting to believe they'd be together twelve months from now. It was safer not to look ahead with Thorne, to live for the moment, but she couldn't help herself.

"Are you hungry?" he asked next.

"Famished." She hadn't eaten anything since early afternoon.

"Good. Do you want to order dinner now or would you rather have another drink?"

"Dinner," Cindy told him. "But if you want another drink, don't let me stop you."

He picked up the menu and shook his head. "I had wine and a couple of cocktails before I caught up with you."

Cindy raised her menu and mulled over the information he'd let slip. He'd lost track of the time, he'd claimed. That would be easy enough to do if he'd been having a good time in the company of a beautiful woman. Her earlier suspicions resurrected themselves. Thorne had been with Sheila. He'd brought in the New Year with the other woman when he'd asked to share the moment with her. He hadn't been with Cindy, but with Sheila, the woman whose picture still sat on his desk. She suddenly knew with certainty that the faint scent she'd noted on Thorne's jacket earlier was perfume. *Sheila's* perfume.

All the special excitement she experienced every time she was with Thorne rushed out of her like air from a punctured balloon. She felt wounded. The commotion and noise in the restaurant seemed to fade into nothingness.

"Have you decided?" Thorne asked.

She stared at him blankly, not understanding what he meant until she realized he was inquiring about her dinner selection. "No. What do you suggest?" It astonished her that she could speak coherently. There would be no next year for them—probably not even a next week. She'd be surprised if they made it through dinner.

You're overreacting, she told herself. *He had a drink with another woman. Big deal.* Thorne wasn't her exclusive property. But he'd obviously held Sheila, held her in his arms... even kissed her. He must have, or the cloying scent of expensive perfume wouldn't be on his clothes.

Deliberately she set the menu aside and glared at him.

"Cindy?"

"Yes?" She made a conscious effort to look attentive.

"What's wrong?"

"I'm fine," she lied. How could she be anything close to fine when all her hopes and expectations were crumbling at her feet? When her dreams had become ashes? Again she told herself she was making too much of it. She had little to go on but conjecture, but in her heart she *knew.* Thorne had left her standing in the miserable cold, alone, while he toasted the New Year with Sheila.

"If you'll excuse me a minute, I

think I'd like to freshen up." Somehow she managed to keep her voice level, revealing none of the emotion she felt.

"Of course." He stood when she did, but as she moved to turn away, his hand reached for her, stopping her. "There are tears in your eyes."

She hadn't been aware that she was crying. She rubbed her face. "What would I have to cry about?" The words sounded as if she were riding on a roller coaster, heaving in pitch, squeezing through the tightness that gripped her throat.

"You tell me."

Cindy reached for her coat and purse, the tears flowing in earnest now. That one drink on an empty stomach had gone to her head and she swayed slightly. "I suddenly figured everything out. I lost the feeling in my toes waiting for you."

Thorne blinked. She wasn't making

any sense. "What do your toes have to do with the fact that you're crying?"

She jabbed a finger in his direction. "You…were…with…Sheila, weren't you?"

He gently pushed her down and took his chair again. He wouldn't back down from the fierce anger in her gaze. Thorne realized his mistake—he should've leveled with her earlier. He would have if he hadn't feared exactly this reaction. "Yes, I was with Sheila."

She leaned across the small table, her eyes spitting fire. "For more than an hour I waited in the cold and wind. You let me stand there while you… entertained another woman. You're right, Thorne, you're no Prince Charming."

"At the moment there isn't the faintest resemblance between you and Cinderella, either."

She ignored that. "If I had any

magic left in me, I'd turn you into a frog."

"Then I'd make you kiss me." He loved her. They were actually arguing, laying their feelings on the table, being honest—even if they were talking the language of fairy tales.

"I don't think it would do any good," Cindy said hotly. "Me kissing you, I mean. You'd still be a frog."

"Possibly," he told her with a grin, "but I doubt it."

Cindy bit her lip. Thorne seemed to think this witty exchange was fun while she was devastated. He was so casual about it, and that hurt.

Thorne immediately sensed the change in Cindy. "I didn't want to be with Sheila," he said, his eyes dark and serious. "I begrudged every minute I wasn't with you."

Cindy didn't know what to believe anymore.

"Then why…"

"I was trapped," he said, and his eyes pleaded for understanding. "I would've given anything to welcome the New Year with you. God willing, I will next year."

Hours later, when she crawled into bed, she wasn't any more confident than she'd been in the restaurant. They'd both ordered lobster and talked for hours, their earlier dispute shelved because their time together was too precious to waste. Cindy was astonished by the way they could talk. They liked the same things, shared the same interests, exchanged ideas and lingered over coffee so long that the waitress grew restless. Only then had Cindy and Thorne noticed that they were the only couple left in the restaurant.

"When can I see you again?" he'd asked.

"Soon," she'd promised, buttoning her coat. "I'll contact you."

He hadn't liked that, Cindy could tell. Before they parted, he'd made her promise that she'd get in touch with him. She would.

Now, as early-morning shadows flitted across the walls, Cindy lay in her bed undecided. Because she'd given Thorne her word, she would meet him, but this had to be the end of it. Oh, heavens, how often had she said that? Too often. And each time, walking away from him had become more difficult. Despite their feelings, despite their similarities of preferences and opinions, their worlds were simply too different.

He was so wonderfully good for her and so disastrously bad for her. She didn't know what she should do anymore. Desire was at war with common sense.

Thorne stood on the dock as large sea gulls circled overhead. The Staten

Island ferry, filled with crowds of tourists who'd wanted a closer view of the Statue of Liberty, was slowly advancing toward the pier.

Cindy had said she'd meet him here. She hadn't shown up yet, but it was still too early to be worried. It had been a week since he'd seen her. His fault, not hers. He'd been out of town on business and had returned home to find a note taped to his apartment door. She'd set the time and place for this meeting. How she'd known he'd be free this afternoon was beyond him. But where she got her information no longer concerned him. Seeing her, being with her—that was what mattered. Nothing else did.

He had to find a way to assure her that she was the most important person in his life. The incident with Sheila had been left unsettled between them. Thorne could tell from Cindy's taut features that she wanted to believe that whatever he'd shared with Sheila was over. But he knew she had her doubts, and he couldn't blame her.

Briefly he thought about the large diamond he kept in the safe at his office. He wanted it on her finger, wanted her promise to be his wife, but he couldn't ask her yet. The timing had to be right. When she completely trusted him, when she opened up to him and told him everything about her life, then he could offer her his.

For now, all he could do was love her and dispel her doubts, one at a time. Today he'd come up with a way of doing that.

"Hi." Cindy joined him on the dock. Her hands were in her pockets as she stood there, looking out at the water.

Slow, grateful relief poured over Thorne. She'd come to him. He could relax and smile again.

"Hi, yourself," he responded with

a smile, resisting the urge to take her in his arms.

"How was Kansas City?"

He smiled, because she'd surprised him again. She'd known where he'd been and for how long. "Dull. I wanted to get back to you. Did you miss me?"

Cindy nodded, although she'd rather not admit it. The week they'd spent apart had seemed like a lifetime. For seven days she'd told herself she'd better get used to living without him as the focal point of her existence. "School started again, so I've been busy."

"But you still thought about me?"

Every minute of every day. "Yes," she answered.

The ferry docked and they stood and watched silently as the passengers disembarked.

"I haven't been to the Statue of Liberty in years," he said. "Have you?" It was obvious that something was troubling her. Cindy wasn't this quiet this long, unless she felt anxious or upset.

"No." The wind swirled her hair around her face and she lifted a strand from her cheek.

Thorne studied her. She looked so troubled, so uncertain that he gently pulled her into his embrace, holding her close.

She sighed and leaned against him, relishing his touch after seven long days without him. She wouldn't be the same after Thorne. She'd go on with her life, but she'd never be the same.

"Are you ready to talk?" he asked, raising her chin so she'd meet his eyes.

At one time she had been, but not anymore. They seemed to take one step forward, then quickly retreat two. Just when she was beginning to feel secure about loving him, he'd left her waiting while he was with Sheila. Although he'd repeatedly claimed the other woman meant nothing to him, he continued to keep her picture on his desk. And recently, quite by accident, she'd discovered a receipt from Tiffany's for a diamond ring. If she'd been insecure about her position in Thorne's life before, now she was paranoid.

"Cindy?" he prompted.

Sadly she shook her head, then brightened. "Shall we walk along the water to get in line for the ferry?"

"No."

"You don't want to go?"

"I have a surprise for you."

"A surprise?" Her heart rocketed to her throat.

He reached for her hand. "We're going someplace special today."

"Where?"

"That's the surprise." He smiled at her and tightened his hand on hers. "My car's down the street."

"Your car?"

"We can't get to...this place by subway."

Despite her reservations, Cindy laughed. "I don't really like surprises."

"This one you will." His fingers tightened around hers. "I promise." After today, Cindy would be sure of her position in his life.

"Is this...someplace I want to go?"

"Now, that may be in question, but you've already agreed."

"I did? When?"

Thorne kissed the tip of her nose. "The night we met."

Cindy shuffled through her memories and came up blank. "I don't recall agreeing to anything."

Thorne pretended shock, then shook his head in mock despair. "How quickly they forget."

"Thorne!" He led her up the street.

"This isn't anyplace fancy, is it?" She wore jeans, a pink turtleneck sweater and loafers with hot pink socks.

"You're perfect no matter what you wear."

"I suppose this is some fancy restaurant where everyone else will be dressed up."

"No restaurant."

"But we are eating?" She hoped they were. As usual, she was starving.

She walked trustfully beside him, despite her reservations about his "surprise." Why, oh, why did it always happen like this? She'd be so uneasy, so certain nothing would ever work between them, and after ten minutes with Thorne, she'd gladly hand over her soul. The thought of being separated from him was unthinkable. She was crazy in love with this man.

"Are you worried about your stomach again?"

"Don't worry, it's something lobster will cure," she joked and was rewarded with a smile.

Cindy would've bet Thorne drove a Mercedes in a subdued shade of gray or steely blue. She was wrong—his car was a Corvette, bright red and so uncharacteristic of him that she stood with her hands on her hips and shook her head.

"I bought it on impulse," he said a bit sheepishly, holding open the passenger door.

She climbed inside, and when she had trouble with the seat belt, Thorne leaned over and snapped it in place. He teased her unmercifully about her lack of mechanical ability, then kissed her soundly when she blushed.

Once they were on the Jersey turnpike, Cindy grew all the more curious. "Just how many days will we be traveling?"

"Forty-five minutes," he answered.

"That long, huh? Aren't you going to give me any clues?"

"Nope. Not any more than I already have."

He was in such a good mood that it was impossible to be serious. Soon they were both laughing, and Cindy didn't notice when he exited the freeway. He drove confidently through a neighborhood of luxurious homes.

"This must be quite some place."

"Oh, it is," he said.

When he turned into a long circular driveway that curved around a huge water fountain, Cindy's curiosity was even sharper. She'd never seen a more opulent home. Huge white pillars dominated the entrance. It looked like something out of *Architectural Digest*.

"Wow." She couldn't find any other word to describe it.

The front door opened and a lovely gray-haired woman came out to greet

Thorne. The older woman's gaze rested on Cindy, and although she revealed little emotion, Cindy had the impression the woman disapproved of her.

Thorne got out of the car and hurried over to kiss the woman on the cheek.

A rock settled in the pit of Cindy's stomach as Thorne opened her door and offered his hand to help her out.

"Cindy," he said, "I'd like you to meet my mother."

Nine

Cindy's introduction to Thorne's parents was strained at best. She was enraged that he'd bring her to his family home without any warning or preparation. Even worse, he'd informed her that what she was wearing was perfectly fine. He couldn't have been more wrong. Jeans and a turtleneck sweater weren't acceptable if Gwendolyn Prince's frown told Cindy anything. Cindy would've been more comfortable being granted an unexpected audience with the pope.

Seated beside Thorne in the extravagant living room, Cindy held the stem of a crystal wineglass between her fingers. Although Thorne's mother was subtle about it, Cindy could feel the other woman studying her. His father's gray eyes sparkled with undisguised delight. He, at least, seemed to be enjoying this farce.

"Where was it you said you met?" the elder Thorne asked.

"The company Christmas party."

Cindy let Thorne answer for her. Her mouth was dry, and she wasn't sure her tongue would cooperate if she tried to speak.

"So you're employed by Oakes-Jenning?"

This time the question was shot directly at Cindy.

"Dad," Thorne interrupted smoothly. "I think I'd like a refill." He held out his glass to his father, who stood and poured the wine.

The elder Prince held the bottle out

to Cindy, but she refused with a shake of her head. If there was ever a time she needed to keep her wits about her, it was now. The minute she was alone with Thorne, she'd let him know what she thought of his "surprise."

"I don't believe I caught your last name," his mother said smoothly.

"Territo. Cindy Territo." Her voice came out more like a croak.

"That sounds ethnic," Thorne's mother commented.

"It's…" Cindy began.

"Italian," Thorne finished.

"I see." His mother obviously didn't.

Cindy watched as the older woman downed the remainder of her wine. She appeared to be as uneasy as Cindy.

"Thorne tells me you're a student?" His father continued the inquisition.

"Yes, I'm studying computer programming."

This, too, was news to Thorne.

He knew Cindy was uncomfortable answering all these questions. He'd asked his parents to make her feel welcome, but he should've known better than to suggest they not intimidate her with rounds of inquiries. His father was too cagey to let the opportunity pass. Thorne reached for Cindy's hand and was astonished to discover that her fingers were cold as ice.

"I'm sure Cindy is equally curious about us," Thorne said, squeezing her hand reassuringly. "Why don't we ask what she'd like to know about us?"

"I...know everything I need to," she murmured with a feeble smile. The instant the words were out, Cindy wanted to grab them back, realizing she'd said the wrong thing. She'd made it sound as if all she cared about was Thorne's money. Nothing could be less true. She would've fallen in love with Thorne had he sold newspapers on a street corner. Now, in addition to being ill at ease, she was acutely embarrassed.

Dinner didn't help. They sat at a long table with a crystal chandelier she suspected was worth more than her uncle's limousine. Thorne was across from her, making her feel even more alone. His parents were at either end of the long table.

A large goblet of ice stood in front of Cindy, and her mouth was so uncomfortably dry that she picked it up, disappointed to find so little water inside. Thorne's mother gave her a pitying glance and instantly Cindy knew she'd committed some terrible faux pas. Her mortification reached its peak when the maid brought a shrimp cocktail, placing the appetizer inside the glass of ice. She dared not look at Thorne, certain he'd find the entire incident amusing.

"What does your father do?" Gwendolyn asked between bites of succulent shrimp.

Briefly Cindy closed her eyes to gather her composure. She'd already disgraced Thorne with her lack of finesse once and she was afraid she'd do it again. "I'm sorry, but I don't know. He deserted my mother and me shortly after I was born."

"Oh, my dear! How terrible for your mother."

"She's gone as well, isn't she?" Thorne asked. His loving gaze caressed her, his brow furrowed with concern.

"She died when I was five."

"Who raised you?" It was the elder Thorne who questioned her now. From the looks they were giving her, one would've thought she'd been beaten daily and survived on dry bread crumbs tossed under the table.

"My aunt and uncle were kind enough to raise me." Thorne's parents exchanged sympathetic glances. "Believe me," Cindy hurried to add, "there's no need to feel sorry for me. They loved me as they would their own daughter. We're a close-knit family with lots of cousins and other relatives." Her aunt and uncle, however, wouldn't dream of interrogating Thorne the way his parents were questioning her.... Then again, maybe they would. Cindy felt slightly better musing about how her uncle Sal would react to meeting Thorne. The first hint of amusement touched the edges of her mouth. She raised her eyes to meet Thorne's and they shared a brief smile.

Dinner couldn't be over soon enough for Cindy. She ate a sufficient amount to ensure that no one would comment. The prime rib rested like a lead weight in the pit of her stomach. Dessert, a frothy concoction of lime and whipped cream, was a cool respite, and she managed to consume a larger portion of that.

"While the women have their coffee, let me show you my new nine iron." The elder Prince addressed his son.

Thorne turned to Cindy. She nodded, assuring him that she'd be fine alone with his mother. She was confident that Gwendolyn Prince had arranged this time so they could speak frankly, and Cindy was prepared to do exactly that.

The men left the table.

Cindy took a sip of coffee and braced herself. She saw that Gwendolyn's hand trembled slightly and she was reassured to realize that the older woman was just as nervous.

Neither spoke for a long moment.

"Mrs. Prince—"

"Cindy—"

They both began at the same instant and laughed, flustered and uneasy.

"You first, dear," Gwendolyn said.

Cindy straightened the linen napkin on her lap. "I wanted to apologize for drinking out of the wrong glass—" She paused, drew in a deep, steadying breath, deciding to do away with small talk and get to the point. "I believe I know what you want to say, and I couldn't agree with you more. You're absolutely right about me. It's perfectly obvious that Thorne and I aren't suited."

If the older woman's hand had trembled before, now it positively shook. "Why, Cindy, what makes you suggest such a thing?"

"You mean other than my drinking from the shrimp glass?"

The first indication that Thorne's mother was capable of a smile showed on her well-preserved face. "My dear girl, shall I tell you about the time I drank too much wine and told Thorndike's mother that she was a cantankerous old biddy?"

Cindy raised the napkin to her mouth to disguise her laugh. "You actually said that?"

"And he proposed the next day. He told me he needed a wife who could stand up to his mother. I'd been crazy about him for years, you see, and I didn't think he knew I was alive. We'd started dating off and on—mostly off—and our relationship seemed to be moving sideways. That Sunday dinner with his family was the turning point in our courtship."

"And you've enjoyed a happy marriage." Cindy made it a statement.

"For over forty years now."

Silence followed.

"I want you to know that very little of what Thorndike and I say will influence our son. He's always been his own man, and he hasn't brought you here for our approval."

Cindy nodded, agreeing that Thorne wouldn't be intimidated by his family's reservations regarding her. "You don't need to say any more. I understand."

"But I'm afraid that you don't," Gwendolyn said hurriedly. "It's just that Thorne and Sheila seemed to be such an item that both Thorndike and I assumed...well, we naturally thought that he and Sheila...oh, dear, I do seem to be making a mess of this."

"It would only seem natural that they'd get married," Cindy said, understanding completely.

"And then out of the blue, Thorne mentioned meeting you." Gwendolyn looked away and reached for her coffee.

Cindy dropped her gaze. The Christmas Ball and her little charade had clearly upset the family's expectations.

"Thorne thinks very highly of you," Gwendolyn added.

"You and your husband must be special people to have raised a son as wonderful as Thorne." Cindy meant that sincerely. "He's touched my life in ways I'll always value."

"I believe you mean that."

"I do, but I realized early on that I'm not the woman for him. He needs a different type." Although she would've given anything to be wrong, she knew she wasn't.

Gwendolyn's cup clanked against the saucer when she set it down. "I don't suppose you've told Thorne that?"

"Not yet."

"He won't give up on you so easily."

Cindy agreed, remembering the detective he'd hired. "He can be as stubborn as an ornery mule."

Gwendolyn laughed outright. "He's quite a bit like his father."

"I'm doing a poor job of expressing myself," Cindy said, not hiding her pain. "I want to reassure you that I won't upset you or your family further by complicating Thorne's life."

"Oh, dear." Gwendolyn looked startled. "Now that I've met you, I was rather hoping you would."

The words were a soothing balm to Cindy. "Thank you."

"Oh, my." Gwendolyn touched her face with her fingertips. "I wonder if I'm making an idiot of myself again. Thorndike swears I should never drink wine."

"He married you because of it," Cindy reminded the older woman, and they exchanged a smile.

"Thorne would never forgive me if I offended you."

"You haven't."

The men joined them a minute later and Thorne's searching gaze sought out Cindy's. She told him with a smile that everything had gone well between her and his mother and she saw him relax visibly. He'd been worried for nothing. She hadn't been raised in a large family without learning how to hold her own.

Thorne gave his parents a vague excuse and they left shortly afterward. Instead of heading toward the freeway, Thorne drove into a church parking lot and turned off the engine.

"My father was impressed with you."

"I can't imagine why," Cindy told him truthfully.

He ignored that. "What did my mother have to say?"

"What I expected."

"Which was?" he probed.

Cindy shook her head. "We came to an understanding."

"Good or bad?"

"Good. I like her, Thorne. She's straightforward and honest."

He rubbed his hand along the back of her neck. "So are you, my love," he said softly and directed her mouth to his, kissing her hungrily.

"So, Cindy Territo, it wasn't such a hard thing to reveal your name, was it?" He brushed his mouth over hers.

"No." Nothing was difficult when she was in his arms. Since the Christmas Ball, she'd allowed his touch to confuse the issue. She'd be so certain of what she had to do, and then he'd kiss her and she'd fall at his feet. It wasn't fair that he had such an overwhelming effect on her. She wasn't weak-willed, nor was her character lacking. She hadn't once suspected that love would do this to a person.

Her aunt was knitting in front of the television set when Cindy let herself into the apartment. Cindy glanced at her, said nothing and moved into the kitchen. Theresa put down the yarn and needles and followed her niece.

"So how was the Statue of Liberty?"

"We didn't go there." Her voice was strained with emotion.

"Oh." Her aunt opened the oven door and basted the turkey roasting inside. "So where'd you go?"

"Thorne took me to meet his family."

Surprised, Theresa let the oven door close with a bang. "His family? You must mean a great deal to him. So how did the introductions go?"

Cindy took a pitcher of orange juice from the refrigerator and poured herself a glass, but not because she was thirsty. She was merely looking for something, anything, to occupy her hands. "I met his mother and father and…nothing."

"'Nothing'? What do you mean?"

Theresa knew her too well for

Cindy to try to fool her. She set the glass of juice on the kitchen table and slumped into a chair, burying her face in her hands.

Theresa patted her shoulder gently. "Love hurts, doesn't it, honey?"

"I've been fooling myself.... It's just not going to work. I made such an idiot of myself—and everyone was so nice. Thorne pretended not to notice, and his mother told me she'd done silly things in her life, too, and his father just looked at me like I was this amusing alien from outer space. I could have died."

"I'm sure that whatever you did wasn't as bad as you think."

"It was worse!" she cried.

"Right now you think it is," Theresa said calmly. "Give it a year or so and you'll look back and laugh at yourself."

Cindy couldn't visualize laughing about anything at the moment. She was hurting too much. She raised her head, sniffling.

"I've decided I'm not going to see him again," Cindy said with iron determination, promising herself as well as informing her aunt. "It isn't going to work, and confusing the issues with love won't change a thing."

"Did you tell Thorne that?"

Miserably, Cindy shook her head. "I didn't want to invite an argument." She refused to spend their last minutes together debating her decision. Thorne had taken her to meet his family to show how easily she'd fit in, and the opposite had proven true. She'd enjoyed his parents. She couldn't imagine not liking the two people most influential in Thorne's upbringing. They were decent folks, but Cindy had known the minute she'd walked inside their home that the chasm that divided their lifestyles was too wide to ever bridge.

She glanced around the Territo family kitchen at the pine table with its plain wooden chairs that had once belonged to her grandmother. There were no plush Persian carpets or Oriental rugs beneath it, only worn hardwood floors. Their furniture was simple, as were their lives. Comparing the two families would be like trying to...to mix spaghetti sauce and rough red wine with lobster and champagne.

Before they parted, Thorne had asked to meet her again. Distraught and too weak to argue with him, Cindy had agreed. Now she was sorry.

"The man's in love with you," Theresa said.

"But encouraging him will only hurt him more."

Theresa sadly shook her head. "Are you saying you don't love him?"

"Yes!" Cindy shouted, then winced at the searing look her aunt gave her. "I love him," she admitted finally, "but that doesn't make everything right. Some things in life were meant to be. Others won't ever work out."

Her aunt's expression was troubled. "You're old enough to know what you want. I'm not going to stand here and argue with you. Besides, anything I say is unlikely to change your mind. But I want you to know that you're a marvelous girl and a man like Thorndike Prince wouldn't fall in love with you if you weren't."

Cindy shrugged helplessly. For now he might have convinced himself that he loved her, but later, after he knew her better, he'd regret his love. Because of their unusual circumstances, he looked upon her as a challenge.

She'd made her decision, and although it was the most difficult thing she'd ever done, she was determined to stick by it.

"Yes?" Thorne flipped the intercom switch, his eyes still on the report he was studying. Interruptions were part of his day and he'd grown accustomed to doing several things at once.

Ms. Hillard cleared her throat. "Your mother is here."

Thorne groaned inwardly. He might be able to have Ms. Hillard fend off unexpected visits from Sheila, but his mother wouldn't be put off by her excuses. He sighed. "Go ahead and send her in."

"Thorne." His mother sauntered into the office, her expression resolutely cheerful.

He stood and kissed her on the cheek, already guessing that she was concerned about something. "To what do I owe this pleasure?" She unbuttoned her coat and he saw that she wore her diamond necklace. Absently Thorne wondered how Cindy would look in diamonds. No, he decided, with her blond hair, he'd buy her emeralds. He'd give her emeralds—earrings and a necklace—as an engagement present when they set their wedding date. He'd have her pearl comb repaired, too. He was anxious to give her all the things she deserved. She'd given him so much in so little time that it would take a lifetime to repay her.

"I was in town and thought I'd let you take me to lunch."

His mother had obviously taught Sheila that trick. "What about Dad?"

"He's tied up in a meeting."

"Ah." Understanding came.

"Besides, I wanted to talk to you."

Thorne bristled, automatically suspicious of her intentions. His mother wanted to discuss Cindy. He sighed, sensing an argument.

"What's the name of that nice little restaurant you like so well?" his mother asked, rearranging the small items on his desk, irritating him further.

"The Corner Bistro."

"Right. Oh. I made reservations at the Russian Tea Room."

Thorne managed to nod. It didn't matter where or what they ate as long as the air was cleared when they finished.

Half an hour later, Thorne studied his mother as they sat in a plush booth in the Russian Tea Room. Methodically she removed her white gloves one finger at a time. He knew her well enough to realize she was stalling.

"You wanted to say something, Mother?" He had no desire to delay the confrontation. If she disapproved of Cindy, he'd prefer to have it out in the open and dealt with quickly. Not that anything she said would alter his feelings toward the woman he loved. He'd prefer it if his family approved, but he wouldn't let them stand in his way.

"Sheila phoned me this morning and I'm afraid I may have done something you'd rather I hadn't." She sent him an apologetic glance and reached for the menu.

Thorne's fingers tightened around his water glass. "Perhaps you should start at the beginning."

"The beginning... Well, yes, I suppose I should." She set the menu aside. "I think you already know that I've had my reservations about Cindy."

"Listen, Mother, I need to tell you that your feelings about Cindy mean very little to me. I love her and, God willing, I plan to marry her and—"

"Please, allow me to finish." She silenced him with a look she hadn't used since his youth. Her words were sharp. "As it happens, I find your Cindy a delight."

"You do?"

"Don't be a ninny! She's marvelous. Now stop acting so surprised." She shook her head lightly. "I thought at first that she might be too shy and retiring for you, which put me in a terrible position, since I doubted you'd care one way or another what I thought of her. But as it happens, I like her. The girl's got pluck."

"Pluck?"

"Yes. I'm pleased that you have the good sense to want to marry her."

Thorne was so astonished he nearly slid out of the booth and onto the floor. "I have every intention of making her my wife as soon as possible. She may put up a fight, but I'm not taking no for an answer."

His mother made a production of straightening the silverware, aligning each piece just so. "Well, dear, there may be a small problem."

"Yes?"

"Sheila seems quite broken up by the news that I'm giving Cindy my wholehearted approval. Mentioning that you'd brought her by to meet your father and me might not have been my smartest move. I had no idea Sheila would react so negatively. I'm afraid the girl may try to create problems for you."

"Let her." Thorne dealt with sensitive situations every day. He could handle Sheila. He'd calm her and end their relationship on a friendly note. "Don't worry, Mother, Sheila's been well aware of my feelings for Cindy for quite some time."

"She seemed to think you'd change your mind."

Thorne's mouth thinned with impatience. "She knows better."

"I'm worried about her, Thorne. I want you to talk to her."

Thorne ran his fingers along the fork tines. "Okay. I'm not sure it'll help. I regret any emotional trauma I may have caused her, but I'm not going to do anything other than talk to her."

"Do it soon."

Thorne agreed, elated with his family's acceptance of Cindy. He recalled the look on her face when he'd left her. She'd clung to him and kissed him with such fervor it had been difficult to leave. He thought about Cindy as his wife and the years that stretched before him—a lifetime of happiness and love. Even though he'd considered marrying Sheila at one point, he'd never thought about their future the way he did with Cindy, plotting the events of their lives.

"I'm seeing her tomorrow."

"Sheila?" his mother inquired.

He shook his head. "No, Cindy."

"But you will talk to Sheila? I'm afraid she might do...something silly."

"I'll speak to her," Thorne promised, determined to put an end to his relationship with the other woman.

Thorne stared at the wall clock in the lobby of the American Museum of Natural History. Cindy was half an hour late. It wasn't like her not to be punctual and he was mildly surprised. He had every minute of their evening planned. Dinner. Drinks. Dancing. Then they'd take a walk in Central Park and he'd bring out the engagement ring. Tonight was it.

All day he'd rehearsed what he was going to say. First, he'd tell her how knowing her had changed his life. It wasn't only singing in the shower and noticing the birds, either. Before she'd walked into his life, he'd fallen into a rut. His work had become meaningless, merely occupying his time. He'd lost his direction.

But her laughter and her smile had lifted him to the heavens, given him hope. He'd tell her that he'd never thought he'd experience the kind of love he felt for her. It had caught him unawares.

Naturally she'd be surprised by

the suddenness of this proposal. She might even insist on an extended engagement. Of course, he hoped they could set the date immediately and begin to make the necessary arrangements for their wedding—a church wedding. He didn't want any rushed affair; when he made his vows to Cindy he wanted them spoken before God, not some fly-by-night justice of the peace. He intended their vows to last a lifetime.

Growing impatient, Thorne pulled the newspaper from his briefcase. Maybe if he read, the snail's pace minutes would go by faster. He scanned the business news and reached for the front page when the society section slipped to the floor.

Thorne retrieved it and was astonished to find Sheila's face smiling at him benignly. Interested, he turned the page right side up and read the headlines.

SHEILA MATHEWSON AN-
NOUNCES PLANS TO MARRY
THORNDIKE PRINCE.

Thorne roared to his feet. The paper
in his hand was crumpled into a wad-
ded mass. So *this* was what his mother
had come to prepare him for.... And
worse, this was the reason Cindy
hadn't shown up.

Ten

The minute Cindy walked into the
apartment, Aunt Theresa and Uncle
Sal abruptly cut off their conversation.
Cindy studied their flushed faces; it
wasn't difficult to ascertain that they'd
been in the midst of a rousing argument. When Cindy arrived, they both
seemed to find things to do. Her aunt
opened the refrigerator and brought
out a head of lettuce and her uncle
reached for a deck of cards, shuffling
them again and again, his gaze on his
hands.

"I'll be in my room," Cindy said,

granting them privacy. She was sorry they were fighting, and although it was uncommon, she knew from experience that it was best to let them resolve their differences without interference from her.

Sitting on the edge of her bed, Cindy eyed the clock. Thorne would be heading for the museum by now, anticipating their meeting. Only she wouldn't be there. She'd allowed him to think she'd agreed to this date, but she hadn't confirmed anything.

Coward! her mind accused her. But she had no choice, Cindy argued back. Every time she was with Thorne, her objections melted like snow under a springtime sun. She was so confused, she didn't know what she wanted anymore. Oh, she loved Thorne. But he was so easy to love. It would be far more difficult *not* to care for him.

Shaking her head vigorously, Cindy decided she couldn't leave Thorne waiting. That was silly and childish. It simply wasn't in her to let him waste his time worrying. She'd go to him and do her utmost to explain. All she'd ask him for was some time apart. A chance to test their feelings. Everything had happened so quickly that it would be wrong to act impulsively now. True love could wait, she'd tell him. A month was what she planned to suggest. Just a month. That didn't seem so long. Thorne would have to promise not to see her until Valentine's Day. If he truly cared for her, he'd agree to that.

Once she'd made her decision—the third one in as many days—she acted purposefully. She had her scarf wrapped around her neck by the time she entered the kitchen. She paused to button her coat.

Her uncle took one look at her and asked, "Where are you going?"

Sal so rarely questioned her about

anything that his brusque inquiry took her by surprise. "I'm… The museum."

"You're not meeting that Prince fellow, are you?"

Her aunt pinched her lips together tightly and slammed the kitchen drawer closed, obviously annoyed by Sal's interrogation.

Cindy's gaze flew from Theresa back to her uncle. "I, uh, yes, I planned to meet Thorne there."

"No."

"No? I don't understand."

"I don't want you to have anything to do with that rich, spoiled kid."

"But, Uncle Sal—"

"The discussion is closed." Sal's hand pounded the tabletop, upsetting the saltshaker.

Cindy gasped and took a step backward. "I'm twenty-five years old! It's a little late to be telling me I can't meet someone."

"You are never to see that man again. Is that understood?"

"Cindy is more than old enough to make up her own mind," Theresa inserted calmly, her back to her husband.

"You keep out of this."

"So the big man thinks he can speak with the authority of a supreme court judge," Theresa taunted, her face growing redder by the second. "Well, I say Cindy can meet her Prince anytime she wishes."

"And I say she can't!" Sal yelled.

"Uncle Sal, Aunt Theresa, please…"

"He's not good enough for you," Sal said, more calmly this time. "Not nearly good enough for our Cindy."

"Oh, Uncle Sal—"

"Cindy…"

The compassion in her aunt's eyes was so strong that Cindy forgot what she wanted to say.

The room went still. Her uncle

stared at the floor and Theresa's eyes glistened with tears.

"Something happened." Cindy knew it without a doubt. "It's Thorne, isn't it?"

Her aunt nodded, her troubled gaze avoiding Cindy's.

"Is he hurt?" She felt alarm bordering on panic. "Oh, you must tell me if he's injured. I couldn't bear it if he—"

"The man's a no-good bum," Sal interrupted. "You're best rid of him."

It was all so confusing. Everyone seemed to be speaking in riddles. She glanced from her uncle back to her aunt, pleading with them both to explain and to put an end to this nightmare of fear.

"I think we'd better tell her," Theresa said softly.

"No!" Sal insisted.

"Tell me what?"

"It's in the paper," Theresa said gently.

"I said she doesn't need to know," Sal shouted, taking the evening paper and stuffing it in the garbage.

"Uncle Sal!" Cindy pleaded. "What is it?"

Theresa crossed the room and reached for Cindy's hand. The last time Cindy could remember seeing her aunt look at her in exactly that way had been when she was a child, and Theresa had come to tell the five-year-old that her mother had gone to live in heaven.

"What is it?" Cindy asked, her voice low and weak. "He's not dead. Oh, no. Don't tell me he's dead."

"No, love," her aunt said softly.

Some of the terrible tension left Cindy's frozen limbs.

Theresa closed her eyes briefly and glanced over her shoulder to her husband. "She'll find out sooner or later. It's better she hear it from us."

For a moment it seemed as if Sal

was going to argue. His chest swelled, then quickly deflated. He looked so unlike his robust, outgoing self that Cindy couldn't imagine what was troubling him.

"Sal read the announcement in the paper and brought it to me."

"The announcement?" Cindy asked. "What announcement?"

"Thorne's marrying—"

"—some high-society dame," Sal broke in. He shook his head regretfully as though he would've done anything to have spared Cindy this.

"But I don't understand," Cindy murmured.

"It was in the society pages."

"Sheila?"

Her aunt nodded.

Cindy sank into a kitchen chair, her legs unable to support her. "I'm sure there's some mistake. I... He took me to meet his family."

"He was using you." Sal came to

stand behind her. He patted her shoulders awkwardly, trying to comfort her. "He was probably using his family to give you the impression that he was serious so he could get you into bed."

"No!" Cindy cried. "No, it was never like that. Thorne didn't even suggest...not once."

"Then thank God. Because it's where he was leading. He's a smart devil, I'll say that for him."

Theresa claimed the chair next to Cindy and took her numb fingers, rubbing them. "I refused to believe it myself until Sal showed me the article. But there it was, bold as can be. It's true, Cindy."

Cindy nodded, accepting what her family was telling her. No tears burned for release. No hysterical sob rose up within her. She felt nothing. No pain. No sense of betrayal. No anger. Nothing.

"Are you going to be all right?" Theresa asked.

"I'll be fine. Don't worry. It was inevitable, you know. I think I knew it from the beginning. Something deep inside me always realized he could never be mine."

"But...oh, Cindy, I can hardly believe it myself."

Cindy stood and hugged her aunt close. "You fell for the magic," she whispered. "So did I for a while. But I'm not really Cinderella and Thorne isn't really a prince. It had to end sometime."

"I hurt so much for you!" Theresa whispered.

"Don't. I'm not nearly as upset as you think," Cindy told her. "I'm going to study for a while." Cindy was fighting off the terrible numbness, knowing she had to do something. Anything. Otherwise she'd go crazy.

Sal slipped an arm around his wife and Theresa pressed her head to his shoulder. "Okay," Sal told his niece softly. "You hit those books and you'll feel better."

Cindy walked back to her room and closed the door. It seemed so dingy inside. Dingy and small. She didn't feel like studying, but she forced herself to sit on the bed and open her textbook. The words blurred, swimming in and out of focus, and Cindy was shocked to realize she was crying.

"I want a retraction and I want it printed in today's paper," Thorne stormed at the society-page editor. The poor woman was red with indignation, but Thorne was beyond caring.

"I've already explained that we won't be able to do that until tomorrow's paper," the woman said for the sixth time.

"But that could be too late."

"I apologize for any inconvenience this may have caused you, Mr. Prince, but we received Ms. Mathewson's announcement through the normal channels. I can assure you this kind of thing is most unusual."

"And you printed the wedding announcement without checking with the alleged groom?"

The woman sat at her desk, holding a pencil at each end with a grip so hard it threatened to snap. "Let me assure you, Mr. Prince, that in all my years in the newspaper business, this is the first bogus wedding announcement that's ever crossed my desk. In the past there's never been any need to verify the event with the, uh, alleged groom—or bride for that matter."

"Then maybe you should start."

"Maybe," she returned stiffly. "Now, if you'll excuse me, I've got work to do."

"You haven't heard the end of this," Thorne said heatedly.

"I don't doubt it," the editor responded.

Thorne did an abrupt about-face and left the newspaper office, unconcerned with the amount of attention his argument had caused.

On the street, he caught the first taxi he could flag down and headed back to the office. As it was, he was working on a tight schedule. He'd already attended an important meeting early that morning—one he'd tried to postpone and couldn't. The minute he was free, he'd had Ms. Hillard contact the PI, Mike Williams, and he'd paced restlessly until he'd learned that Mike was out of town on a case and not expected back for another week.

The detective could well be his only chance of finding Cindy. Mike had gotten close once, but after Cindy had shown up outside his office building,

Thorne had done as she requested and asked Mike to halt his investigation. After all, he'd gotten what he'd wanted—Cindy was back. Now he wished he'd pursued it further. He had no more chance of finding her now than when she'd left him the night of the Christmas Ball.

A feeling of desperation overpowered him. When Cindy hadn't appeared at the museum, Thorne had spent the evening calling every Territo in the phone book—all fifty-seven—to no avail. By the time he'd finished, he was convinced she'd given him a phony name. Either that, or she had an unlisted number. From there he had no more leads.

Thorne dreaded returning to his office. No doubt there'd be enough phone and e-mail messages to occupy his afternoon—and he was supposed to be working on a merger! Thank goodness it was almost completed.

Still, this was not the week to be worrying about Cindy. He had neither the time nor the patience to be running around New York looking for her.

Ms. Hillard stood up when Thorne entered his office.

"Yes?" he barked, and was instantly contrite.

"Mr. Jenning would like to talk to you when you have a moment." Her eyes didn't meet his and Thorne felt a twinge of guilt. He'd been abrupt with her just now, but it was tame in comparison to his treatment of Sheila. She'd been to see him first thing that morning and he'd hardly been able to look at her as the anger boiled within him. The woman had plotted to ruin his life. It was her fault that he couldn't locate Cindy. He'd said things to Sheila that he'd never said to anyone. He regretted that now.

Perhaps he might have found it in his heart to forgive her, but she'd revealed no contrition. It almost seemed as if she was proud of what she'd done. He hadn't been the only one to lose his composure; Sheila had called Cindy the most disgusting names. Even now, hours later, Thorne burned with outrage.

In the end, he'd ruthlessly pointed at the door and asked her to leave. Apparently she'd realized her mistake. She began sobbing, ignoring his edict. He'd told her firmly that he planned to marry Cindy and nothing she could do would change his plans. Then, not knowing what else to do, Thorne had called in his secretary.

"Ms. Hillard," he'd said, his eyes silently pleading with the older woman. "It seems Ms. Mathewson needs to powder her nose. Perhaps you could show her the way to the ladies' room."

"Of course."

Mentally Thorne made a note to give his secretary a raise. The older woman had handled the delicate situation with finesse. Tenderly she'd placed her arm around the weeping Sheila's shoulders, and with nothing more than a few whispered words she'd directed her away from Thorne's desk and out of his office.

Sighing, Thorne sank down in his chair and looked over his messages. Paul Jenning had asked to see him, probably about his upcoming retirement and his not-so-secret proposal that Thorne succeed him. But even though this was what Thorne had always wanted, he couldn't feel excited about it. If only he knew how to contact Cindy...

"Have you been in *his* office yet?"

Cindy didn't need to guess whose office Vanessa was referring to. Her coworker hadn't stopped talking about Thorne from the moment Cindy had arrived for work. "Not yet."

"Are you going in there?"

"Vanessa, it's my job—nothing more and nothing less."

The other woman pushed her cleaning cart down the hallway, casting Cindy a worried glance now and then. "How can you be so calm? Aren't you tempted to booby-trap his desk or something? As far as I'm concerned, Prince is the lowest form of life. He's lower than low. Lower than scum."

Cindy pressed her lips together and said nothing.

"You're taking this much too calmly."

"What do you want me to do?" Cindy asked, losing patience.

"I don't know," Vanessa returned. "Cry, at least. Weep uncontrollably for a day or two and purge him from your system."

"It would take more than a good bout of crying to do that," Cindy mused. "What else?"

Vanessa looked confused. "I'd think you'd want to hate him."

Cindy wasn't allowed that luxury, either. "No, I can't hate him." Not when she loved him. Not when she wished for his happiness with every breath. Not when everything within her was grateful for the short time they'd shared. "No," she repeated softly. "I could never hate him."

They paused outside Thorne's office. "You want me to clean it for you?"

"No." Cindy didn't need to think twice about it. From this night forward, Thorne's office would be the only contact she had with him. It was far too much—and yet, not nearly enough.

"You're sure?"

"Positive."

The outer office, which Ms. Hillard occupied, was neat, as always, but Cindy brushed her feather duster over the desk and around the computer keyboard. Next, she plugged in the vacuum cleaner. With a flip of the switch it roared to life, but she hadn't done more than a couple of swipes when it was suddenly switched off. Surprised, Cindy whirled around to discover Thorne holding the plug in his hand.

"Can't this wait?" he snapped, tossing the plug onto the carpet. "In case you hadn't noticed, I'm working in here."

Cindy was too stunned to react. It was obvious he hadn't even looked at her. She was, after all, only the cleaning woman.

She turned, prepared to leave without another word, but in her rush, she bumped against the side of the desk and knocked over a stack of papers. They fluttered down to the carpet like autumn leaves caught in a gust of wind.

"Of all the inept…"

Instantly, Cindy crouched down to pick them up, her shaking fingers working as quickly as she could make them cooperate.

"Get out before you do any more damage or I'll have you fired."

Cindy reared up, her eyes spitting fire. "How *dare* you speak to me or anyone else in that demeaning tone?" she shouted. She had the satisfaction of watching Thorne's jaw sag open. "You think that because you're Mr. Almighty Vice President you can treat other people like they're your servants? Well, I've got news for you, Thorndike Prince. You can't have me fired because—I quit!" With that she removed the feather duster from her pocket, shoved it in his hand and stormed out of his office.

Eleven

Thorne moved quickly, throwing the feather duster aside and hurrying out of his office. So this was Cindy's terrible secret. He'd never been more relieved about anything in his life. A flash of pinstriped coveralls and red bandana caught his attention in the office across from his own and he rushed in.

"Cindy, you crazy idiot." He took her by the shoulders, whirled her around and pressed her close to hug the anger out of her.

She struggled, her arms flailing ineffectively, but Thorne wasn't about to set her free. Her cries were muffled against his broad chest.

"Honey, don't fight me. I'm sorry—"

She gasped, braced her palms against him and pushed with all her might until she broke free. If Thorne had been surprised to find Cindy cleaning his office, it was an even greater shock to discover that the woman he'd been holding wasn't Cindy.

"I'm not your 'honey,'" Vanessa howled.

"You're not Cindy."

"Any idiot could see that." Disgruntled, she rearranged her bandana and squared her shoulders. "Do you always behave like an ape-man?"

"Where's Cindy?"

"And you're not exactly the love of *my* life, either," Vanessa continued sarcastically.

Thorne rushed from the office and down the hall, stopping to search every room. Cindy was gone. Vanished. This was how it happened every time. Just when he thought he'd found her, she disappeared, sending him into agony until she stumbled into his life again. No more. They were going to settle this once and for all!

He rushed back to the other young woman, leaned both hands against the office doorway and shouted, "Where'd she go?"

"I don't know if I should tell you." She idly dusted the top of Rutherford Hayden's desk, obviously enjoying her moment of glory.

"You—what's your name?"

"Vanessa, if it's any of your business."

Thorne clenched his fists, growing more impatient. He wasn't going to let this impertinent Vanessa person keep him from the woman he loved. "Either you tell me where she is or you're out of here."

"I wasn't all that keen to keep this job anyway," Vanessa said, faking a yawn. She sauntered to the other side of the office. "Do you love her?"

"Yes!"

"If that's the case, then why was your engagement to another woman announced in the paper?"

"Sheila lied. Now, are you going to tell me where Cindy went?"

"So, you aren't going to marry this other woman?"

"That's what I just got through telling you. I want to marry Cindy."

Vanessa raised her index finger to her lips, as if giving the matter consideration. "I suppose I *should* tell you, then."

"Could you do it fast?"

"I was the one who brought Cindy

your picture and told her you might be her prince."

"We'll name our first daughter after you." Thorne said the words from between gritted teeth.

"Fair enough," Vanessa said with a sigh. "Take the elevator all the way to the basement, go left, then at the end of the corridor go left again, and it's the first room on your right. Have you got that?"

"Got it." Thorne took off running. "Left, left, right. Left, left, right," he mumbled over and over while he waited for the elevator. The ride to the basement had never seemed slower, especially when he realized that he had to change elevators on the main floor. When he couldn't locate the service elevator, the security guard, Bob Knight, came to his aid.

Just before the heavy door glided

shut, Thorne yelled, "We'll name one of our children after you, too!"

Cindy was too furious to think straight. She removed her coveralls and flung them carelessly into the laundry bin. "Can't you see I'm working in here," she muttered, sarcastically mimicking Thorne's words. The red bandana followed the coveralls, falling short of the bin, but Cindy couldn't have cared less.

"Cindy."

At the sound of Thorne calling her name, Cindy turned, closed the door and slid the lock into place.

Thorne tried the door, discovered it was locked, then pounded on it with both fists. "Cindy, I know you're in there!"

She refused to answer him.

"Cindy, at least hear me out."

"You don't need to say a word to me, Mr. Almighty Thorndike Prince."

Dramatically she brought the back of her wrist to her forehead. "I suggest you leave before you do any more damage and I'm forced to have you fired." She taunted him with his own threat.

"Cindy, please, I'm sorry. I had no idea that was you."

She reached for her jeans, sliding them over her hips and zipping them up, her hands shaking in her hurry to dress. "I think you're...despicable. Vanessa was right. You are the lowest of the low."

"She'll change her mind. I just promised to name our first daughter after her."

"Oh, stop trying to be clever!"

"Cindy," he tried again, his voice low and coaxing, "hear me out. I've had a rotten day. I was convinced I'd never find you again and one thing after another has gone wrong. You're right, I shouldn't have shouted at you, but please understand. I didn't know you were the cleaning lady."

She rammed her arms into the long sleeves of her sweatshirt and jerked it over her head. "It shouldn't have mattered who I was…as you kept telling me."

"And I meant it. If you'd let me explain…"

"You don't need to explain a thing to me…I'm only the cleaning woman."

"I love you, cleaning woman."

Telling her that was cheating, since he knew the effect it would have on her. Cindy threw open the door and faced him, arms akimbo and eyes flashing. "I suppose you love Sheila, too."

"No, I—"

"Don't give me that. Did you think I'm so socially inept I wouldn't find out about your wedding announcement? I do happen to read the paper now and again."

"Sheila had that published without my knowledge. I have no intention of marrying her. How could I when I'm in love with you?"

That took some of the wind from her sails, as her aunt might have said, and her temper went with it. She closed her eyes and bowed her head. "Don't tell me you love me, Thorne. I don't think I'll be able to leave you if you do."

Thorne reached for her, astonished anew at how right it felt to hold her. He held her tight and sighed in relief. He had his Cindy, his princess, his love, and he wasn't going to lose her again.

"That night was all a game," she whispered. "I never dreamed...never hoped you'd come to care for me."

"The magic never stopped and it never will. You're mine, Cindy Territo. And I'm yours."

"But, Thorne, surely you understand now why I couldn't let you know."

"Do you think it matters that you're a janitor? I love you. I want you to share my life."

Cindy tensed. "Thorne, I'm scared."

"There's no reason to be." His hand smoothed the curls at the back of her head.

"Are you crazy?" Cindy asked with a sobbing laugh. "Look at us."

Thorne blinked.

"You're standing there in your thousand-dollar suit and I'm wearing bargain-basement blue jeans."

"So?"

"So! We're like oil and water. We don't mix."

Thorne smiled at that. "It just takes a little shaking up. You can't doubt that we were meant to be together, Cindy, my very own princess."

"But, Thorne—"

He kissed her then, cutting off any

further objection. His mouth settled firmly over hers; the kiss was both undeniably gentle and magically sweet. When he held her like this, it was easy to believe that everything would always be wonderful between them.

"I want to meet your family."

"Thorne, no." Cindy broke out of his arms, hugging her waist.

He looked puzzled. "Why not?"

"Because—"

"I'll need to meet them sometime."

Her uncle Sal's contorted, angry face flashed before Cindy. She knew he disapproved of Thorne. If Cindy were to bring Thorne to the apartment, Sal would punch first and ask questions later. Any of her uncles would behave the same way. Her family was highly protective of all their loved ones, and there'd have to be a whole lot of explaining before Cindy brought Thorne into their midst.

"Meet them?" Cindy repeated. "Why?"

"Cindy." He held her squarely by the shoulders. "I plan to marry you. If you'll have me, of course."

She stared at him, overwhelmed by happiness—and then immediately swamped by doubts.

"You will be my wife, won't you?"

He asked her with such tenderness that Cindy's eyes brimmed with tears. She nodded wildly. "Yes…"

Thorne relaxed.

"No," she said quickly, then covered her face with both hands. "Oh, good grief, I don't know!"

"Do you love me?"

Her response was another vigorous nod.

"Then it's settled." He removed her hands from her face and kissed her eyes and her nose. Then his lips descended slowly toward her mouth, pausing at her earlobe, working their way across the delicate line of her jaw....

"But, Thorne, nothing's settled. Not really. We... I need time."

"Okay, I'll give you time."

The organ music vibrated through the church. Cindy stood at the back of St. Anthony's and her heart went still as the first bridesmaid, holding a large bouquet of pink rosebuds, stepped forward. The second and the third followed. Cindy watched their progress, and her heart throbbed with happiness. This was her wedding day and within the hour she would experience the birth of her dreams. She would become Thorne's wife. Somehow they'd crossed every hurdle. She'd claimed she needed time. He'd given it to her. She'd been so sure her family would object, but with gentle patience Thorne had won over every member. Now it was June and almost six months had passed since the night of the Christmas Ball. Thorne had convinced her the magic of that night would last throughout their lives, and finally Cindy could believe him. There wasn't anything in this world their love couldn't overcome. They'd proved it.

Thorne stood at the altar, waiting for her. His eyes were filled with such tenderness that Cindy had to resist the urge to race into his arms.

His smile lent her assurance. He didn't look the least bit nervous, while Cindy felt as if a swarm of bees was about to invade her stomach. From the first, he'd been the confident one. Always so sure of what was right for them. Never doubting. Oh, how she loved him.

The signal came for four-year-old Carla to join the procession, and dressed in her long lavender gown, the little girl took one measured step after another.

Cindy stood at the back of the church and looked out over the seated guests. To her left were the people who'd loved and nurtured her most of her life. Aunt Theresa sat in the front row, a lace handkerchief in her hand, and Cindy saw her dab away an escaped tear. Cousins abounded. Aunts, uncles, lifelong friends, Vanessa, Bob Knight and others who'd come to share this glorious day. She lifted a hand to the pearl comb Thorne had returned to her. The combs secured her delicate veil. Cindy thought of her mother and how happy she would've been today.

To her right was Thorne's family. Wealthy, cultured, sophisticated. St. Anthony's parking lot had never hosted so many Cadillacs and Mercedes, nor had this humble sanctuary witnessed so many designer dresses and expensive suits. But they'd come, filling the large church to capacity, wanting to meet the woman who was about to marry Thorne Prince.

The organ music reached a crescendo when Cindy stepped onto the trail of white linen that ran the length of the aisle. The train of the satin and lace dress that had been worn by both her mother and her aunt flowed behind her. Cindy walked at a slow and stately pace, each resounding note of the organ drawing her closer to Thorne, her prince, her love.

The congregation stood and Cindy felt a surge of excitement as the faces of those she loved turned to watch her progress.

Thirty minutes later Cindy moved back down the same aisle as Thorne's wife. Family and friends spilled out of the church, crowding the steps. Cindy was repeatedly hugged and Thorne shook hand after hand.

The limousine arrived, and with his guiding hand at her elbow, Thorne led her down the steps and held open the car door.

Almost immediately, he climbed in after her.

"Hello, Mrs. Prince," he whispered, his voice awed. "Have I told you today how much I love you?" he asked.

"You just did that with a church full of witnesses," she reminded him softly. "I do love you, Thorne. There were so many times I didn't believe this day could ever happen, and now that it has, I know how right it is."

He gathered her in his arms and kissed her to the boisterous approval of their guests, who were still watching from the sidewalk.

"Did you see the banner?" Thorne asked, pointing to the church.

"No."

"I think Vanessa had something to do with that."

Cindy laughed. There, above the doors, a banner was hung, the words bold and bright for all the world to read:

CINDY AND HER PRINCE LIVED HAPPILY EVER AFTER.

* * * * *

ESSENTIAL COLLECTION

YES! Please send me the *Essential Collection by Debbie Macomber* in Larger Print. This collection begins with 3 FREE books and 2 FREE gifts in the first shipment, and more free gifts will follow! My books will arrive in 8 monthly shipments until I have the entire 51-book *Essential Collection by Debbie Macomber*. I will receive 2 or 3 FREE books in each shipment and I will pay just $4.99 U.S./$5.89 CDN. for each of the other 4 books in each shipment, plus $2.99 for shipping and handling. *If I decide to keep the entire collection, I'll have paid for only 32 books because 19 books are FREE! I understand that by accepting the 3 free books and gifts places me under no obligation to buy anything. I can always return a shipment and cancel at any time. My free books and gifts are mine to keep no matter what I decide.

261 HCN 1446   461 HCN 1446

Name	(PLEASE PRINT)

Address	Apt. #

City	State/Prov.	Zip/Postal Code

Signature (if under 18, a parent or guardian must sign)

Mail to the Harlequin® Reader Service:
IN U.S.A.: P.O. Box 1867, Buffalo, NY 14240-1867
IN CANADA: P.O. Box 609, Fort Erie, Ontario L2A 5X3

* Terms and prices subject to change without notice. Prices do not include applicable taxes. Sales tax applicable in N.Y. Canadian residents will be charged applicable taxes. This offer is limited to one order per household. All orders subject to approval. Credit or debit balances in a customer's account(s) may be offset by any other outstanding balance owed by or to the customer. Please allow 4 to 6 weeks for delivery. Offer available while quantities last. Offer not available to Quebec residents.

Reader Service.com

Manage your account online!

- Review your order history
- Manage your payments
- Update your address

> *We've designed
> the Harlequin® Reader Service
> website just for you.*

Enjoy all the features!

- Reader excerpts from any series
- Respond to mailings and special monthly offers
- Discover new series available to you
- Browse the Bonus Bucks catalog
- Share your feedback

Visit us at:
ReaderService.com